WITHDRAWN

P9-ASG-746

THE PERMANENCE OF WAVES

THE PERMANENCE OF WAVES

C. J. CLARK

LANGMARC
PUBLISHING

AUSTIN, TEXAS

The Permanence of Waves
Fable and Drawings
by C. J. Clark

The cover photograph of Betty, Margorie and
Fowler D. Brooks was taken at Stony Point on
Battle Lake in Minnesota around 1935.

Copyright © 2006 by C.J. Clark
Illustrations Copyright © 2006 by C.J. Clark
First Printing 2006
Printed in the United States of America

All rights reserved. No part of this book may be reproduced or
transmitted in any form or by any means, electronic or mechanical,
including photocopying, record, or by any information storage and
retrieval system, without the written permission of the publisher,
except for a review. Although the place—Stony Point, Battle Lake,
Minnesota, is a real place, any resembles to actual persons is coinci-
dental.

PUBLISHED BY
LANGMARC PUBLISHING
P.O. Box 90488
AUSTIN, TEXAS 78709-0488
www.langmarc.com

Library in Congress Cataloging: 2006926371
ISBN: 1880292-815

DEDICATION

For Grandpa, who brought us here,
for Grandma, Mother, Dad, Pam, Joe, Jennifer,
and Catherine who believed in it,
and for Scout, who discovered the secret stones

Do you not see
the shimmering stones you took
from beneath sun-bleached docks
lost their dance of light
when placed in drawers forgotten?

Did you not sense
the blue heron lake wore those speckled
stones like brilliant buttons
To hold together
her glistening garment of waves?

Couldn't you instead store
treasured green and maroon flecked stones
somewhere inside you
to dance on your light, in your memories,
leaving the lake
Unbroken?

From "Whispers in the Wind" by Pam Trogolo

TABLE OF CONTENTS

BLUE WATER STONES

Otter Tail County Road 16 was sprinkled with just enough cold rainwater to make it slick for travelers. Especially cyclists. And even worse for an elderly man peddling uphill. The lone cyclist braced himself against the steady pinpricks of water, tipping his cap just over his eyes. He peered out at the bleak landscape, marveling at how May in Minnesota could always manage to hurl the last remnants of winter back at spring. His red flannel shirt and blue jeans were a shock contrast to the gray of the morning. His bones ached, and he was chilled and shivering from the dampness, but he kept peddling. Painstakingly, he climbed the hill passing the town cemetery, which had once been rolling prairie before grave markers began to appear. The graves had tripled in number since he'd first traveled this highway, when it was still a dirt road. But he did not look in that direction. His eyes were fixed on the road ahead of him.

A car sped past him, splashing water. He could see that the car was filled with laughing teenagers.

Thunderous music blared from their open windows, sounding like a car wreck in progress. It dissipated like a muffled scream as they moved further down the road. Sighing, he welcomed the quiet of his bicycle tires on the wet pavement and listened intently to the singing meadow birds. He knew the birds by their individual songs. He knew things that he felt no one cared about anymore.

On both sides of the road there was open land descending into woods that led to a small lake. He would always pause beside the lake because the water was such a brilliant blue. He felt healed just looking at it. He could breathe more deeply. Except for an occasional fishing boat, the little lake was uninhabited by cabins on the shoreline. Even on this dreary May morning, it looked more blue than gray to him.

Taking a sharp breath, he noticed a white-tailed deer lying by the side of the road. He stopped. Slowly he got off his bicycle and moved toward the deer. It was a doe. She had been killed by a car probably earlier that morning. What a waste, he thought, shaking his head and stooping down to run his gnarled hand along the doe's smooth coat. Her coat had already begun to turn to the more reddish color of summer.

The man's legs were stiff, making the task of getting back onto his bicycle almost unbearable. Gradually he resumed his peddling, turning sharply down a gravel road that was so bumpy he considered walking his bike the rest of the way. The Main Camp Road. We used to call it the Main Camp Road, he thought. It was because we came here not to intrude; we came here just to set up camp. We came to build just a few noninvasive cabins by the lake and coexist with the land and with every creature from the weakest to the strongest. He thought of the dead doe with sadness.

He was the last of his generation now. He looked down at the package he carried with him. It contained a loaf of brown bread, a slab of butter wrapped in wax paper, a tin of peaches in heavy syrup, and the day's mail. He'd almost forgotten why he'd made this trip to town. His pace was excruciatingly slow. He gazed with appreciation at the thick deciduous woods on both sides of the road. Patches of early spring green dotted the woods. He became preoccupied with identifying which trees were yet to emerge with emerald leaves that would fill in the gray spaces left by winter.

Eventually the road narrowed and divided into a fork. It still amazed him that a sign had been installed here by the county. Stony Point Trail. Decades had passed without that sign. He turned and applied the brake pedal against the steep downward bend. A rush of rain-scented woods filled his nostrils. It was his favorite aroma in the world. What was distressing was that the scent had somehow become diluted over the years. The trail had once been a tiny grass lane with towering trees and underbrush, crowding it from both sides into a narrow passageway. As he approached the cabin, his pedaling had slowed to nearly a standstill. He was greeted by a boisterous yellow Labrador retriever.

"Hello there, poochie dog!" He patted the joyful dog on the head and looked into her liquid brown eyes. This was a good dog. Folks wondered aloud if he was perhaps too old to own such an energetic dog. But Scout was different. She was gentle, and she seemed even more perceptive than a lot of people he knew. She never chased the chipmunks or squirrels. She just didn't do dog things. And her devotion to him was touching. What would become of her if they had to leave here, he wondered. She followed him into the cabin.

He sat in his old rocker that smelled of wood smoke and moth balls and began to thumb through the stack of mail from town. There were bills and announcements and a letter from his granddaughter, Olive, who lived in Kansas. He held it for a moment, feeling almost too drowsy to read, but he opened it anyway. Her handwriting was childlike for a thirty-year-old woman. He smiled at this, then began to read aloud to Scout since her face was plunked down onto his knee, waiting.

Dearest Grandpa,
    By the time you read this letter, Lottie and I will be on our way there to see you. I hope you are well. I've been worried because I've not heard much from you. I called the neighbors and they told me you are getting along fairly well, but they are so far from you that they see you only once in a while.
    I hope you are considering my offer to come back with us to Kansas. Our house isn't big but you would have your own room across from the bathroom. There are lots of good doctors in Kansas City and there are interesting things to do. You might like it. And of course, Scout is welcome! Lottie loves her dearly. We can talk about this when we get there.
    Well, I have to finish packing and get this mailed. See you soon.
                                            Love, Olive

He folded the letter and closed his eyes. It would be good to see them. Lottie was eight now and her world was changing rapidly, caught up in friends and activities. Her parents had been killed in a car accident leaving Olive, her mother's sister, to care for her, something she had done admirably. His own daughter, Olive's mother, had died years ago from an incurable heart ailment. Olive and Lottie were his only heirs. One day they would inherit this cozy cabin, the beach filled with its large, colorful stones leading to the clear lake, the blue sky, the expanse of wooded land, and every other beloved thing. Would they ever truly appreciate the natural peace and brilliance of it?

Would they ever learn, as he had, to gaze into the silent lake's reflection at sunset and see the world as pure and perfect? Or maybe he saw these things because he was old and had walked these stony shores for so very long. It was a part of him. Like another layer of skin. It just couldn't be described in words. Maybe because it was too simple. You either loved the natural world or you didn't. You either saw the goodness of it or you didn't. You either respected it or you didn't.

He stared out the window at the morning sky. The gray was beginning to break apart into sapphire patches and wisps of lavender clouds. A blue heron glided by. He watched the reflection of it in the water, thinking how unspoiled the image was. It was graceful and serene but when he looked back at the sky, he felt there was something peculiar about the way the heron was flying. Herons rarely seemed uncertain, but this one did. Perhaps it was because of the construction of new cabins and widening of roads at the far end of the lake. The heron's habitat had likely been disrupted.

It was inevitable that, in spite of everything, people would come and go, and in their attempts to extract recreation from the lake and woods they would somehow disturb it. They would disturb a whole world they couldn't even see. Well, maybe he had become a sentimental old fool after all. He chuckled. Scout's tail thumped vigorously against the cold linoleum floor.

The man pried himself up and out of the old rocker, still feeling the ache from his bicycle ride. He shuffled his way to the kitchen and made a mug of instant coffee, black and strong. He blew on the steaming coffee, then took big slurps of it, not caring how loud he sounded. Noticing that the fireplace still had a few orange embers, he stirred them into dancing little flames and added wood. Good solid slow burning ironwood. For a moment he stood mesmerized by the spit and dance of the rekindled fire. Some of the ache in his bones melted away.

In the distance he heard a flock of Canadian geese honking. The sound became louder as the geese got closer, drawing his attention to the lakeshore. The light breeze of morning had begun to develop into a gusty wind causing the lake to become choppy. He watched waves spill onto shore, washing the beach stones into brilliant colors.

Scout loved the stones. It was an odd fascination, really. Sometimes he saw Scout stare at the stones as though she were willing them to acknowledge her, and at other times she would step into the shallow water, dip her nose into the lake, gingerly pick up a stone, then drop it carefully onto the beach with the other stones. The funny thing was, she did this only if she thought he wasn't watching her.

The two of them walked out into the day. Scout bounded ahead, stopping ever so often while he navigated the steep bank leading to the stone beach. A noisy cawing crow announced their presence. Leaning heavily against the oldest stooped cottonwood tree, he decided that he would need to spend the day tidying the cabin for the arrival of his granddaughter and great granddaughter. Not a small task. His housekeeping skills had been rudimentary at best. There were endless stacks of books, winter jackets thrown across the backs of chairs, and clean dishes crowding the countertops ready for his use. There were Scout's dog-haired furniture covers and wood chips to be swept away. Well, perhaps it wasn't all that horrible. He gazed into the old cottonwood's branches, then at the ancient beach stones, momentarily envious of their simplicity.

"No walk today, Scout. We're expecting company," he told the dog who had been anticipating her daily trek to the creek. But the dog bristled and stood rigid, looking away from him towards the cabin. They heard a car door slam.

"Grandpa! We're here! Grandpa!" He followed the dog's gaze to see Lottie racing down the bank towards him. Scout slowly began to wag her tail. Behind Lottie was Olive, who was sprinting towards him. Their momentum was so great that if he hadn't been leaning against the old cottonwood tree, he might have been sent sprawling into the water by their joyful hugs.

"Welcome! Welcome to our Stony Point!" he exclaimed happily. It was what he always said when they came to visit. Our Stony Point. Olive and Lottie had come to expect this greeting.

"You made good time. I just read your letter this morning. The cabin is pretty cluttered, I'm afraid. Not all that much in the way of food either."

"Oh, now don't worry about that," Olive said, winking at Lottie. "We stopped and bought groceries on the way here. Really, we're just glad to be here."

"How long can you stay?"

"Not too long this time, Grandpa, but we can talk about all that later. You look tired. Are you okay?" Olive asked, standing back to study him. She thought he looked frail and drained of color. A sudden gust of wind threatened to throw him off balance. Gently she took his arm and led him away from the stony beach. For an instant, he struggled to keep his footing on the large stones. Olive tightened her grip on his arm.

"Lottie, how do you like school? Are you glad to be almost finished for this year?" he asked in attempt to shift their focus from his momentary weakness.

As they walked together back to the cabin, Olive listened to her grandfather and niece talk enthusiastically about her school work, her plans for the summer, her friends, and her passion for art. He had always had such a keen interest in kids. He'd been a brilliant psychologist and had retired to write books on various topics. The writing had not been overly successful, but he had been very content living here at the lake cabin he and his brother had built over forty years ago. It was a good place.

Olive had been coming here every summer since her childhood, as had her mother. It was somewhat remote, very quaint, and nothing at all like the life she was used to in Kansas City. But it always happened that once she was here, she felt a soothing sort of peace envelop her. She felt as though each breath she took somehow cleansed her soul, like waves washing over stones.

Getting settled took some doing. Olive had to clear counter space, restock the refrigerator, make the beds with clean sheets, and straighten up some of the clutter. She was captivated by the old photographs on the fireplace mantle. A photo of her mother and grandmother were predominantly placed. There were school pictures of Lottie and one of Lottie's mother and father. And there was one of herself taken after her divorce. She thought she looked gaunt and preoccupied. The photo was taken long before Lottie had come to live with her.

Olive spent some time dusting and sweeping up wood chips and returning books to the bookshelves. When she was finished cleaning, she realized it was late enough for supper, so she busied herself preparing a meal for the three of them. It was then that she silently rehearsed what she planned to say to her grandfather. She dreaded the conversation. It would be such a turning point. She had always idolized her grandfather. It didn't seem natural to tell him what she thought would be best for him.

As daylight slipped into the cold darkness of night, a brisk lake wind began to gust around the cabin. Olive said nothing until Lottie went to bed. Her grandfather sat in his old worn rocker, drumming his fingers on the big wooden arms of the chair. A roaring fire in the fireplace warmed the room. They listened in silence to the crackle and hiss of it. Finally she spoke.

"Grandpa, have you given any thought to coming with us to Kansas?"

She moved closer to the edge of her chair.

"No, Olive. I can't say that I have. Although I do appreciate the offer." He smiled at her as though that would be the end of the discussion.

"But listen, Grandpa, I fixed a room for you. It's the big corner room with the south and east windows. There's that beautiful old mimosa tree on the south side. Remember all those little wren houses you built? I hung them in that tree. And during the day you'll have the whole house to yourself. I think you'll find that Kansas City is a good place to live. There's a church down the street from us and a branch library, too. And we're really close to doctors and a hospital. Plus, there are a lot of things to do. If you want to get out and walk, there's a park nearby. It's very peaceful." She realized that she was babbling like a salesperson and stopped talking.

"It sounds very nice, Olive. I know you're happy there. And Lottie, too. But this is my home. I'm not sure I have the words to describe how I feel about this land. It's no ordinary lake cabin in the woods. Besides, Olive, I'm very set in my ways. You would find me quite annoying after a while." He chuckled, reaching down to pet Scout who stared at him adoringly.

Olive didn't laugh. She felt frustrated and decided to try a different approach. "The thing is, I worry about you up here all by yourself. Oh, I know you have neighbors who check on you but, Grandpa, do you think it's a good idea to ride your bicycle all the way to town? I mean, you have the car. And what about staying warm or just getting around? What if you fall or get sick? Your phone doesn't even have an answering machine. And..."

For a moment the two of them sat listening to the wind howling outside . They could hear waves crashing against the shore, while inside, the cabin glowed with warmth and memories reaching across generations. Olive watched her grandfather rest his head against the back of the rocking chair.

"Grandpa, I'm just saying, you're not getting any younger." Her tone was becoming more pleading. "I think it would be best if you lived where someone could make sure you were safe."

He leaned forward and patted her hand the way he had when she was a child.

"Olive, do you remember that drawer in your room here, the one where you put all the pretty stones and other things you collected from the beach when you were little?"

"Yes, I guess so, but..." She didn't understand the shift in conversation. It irritated her. She would not look at him.

"All those things were treasures to you, each special in its own way, worthy of collecting and worthy of putting away for safekeeping. But in time you forgot about them, and so, they still sit in the drawer, useless and waiting, out of their element." He waited for her to look at him.

"But what does that have to do with what I'm saying?" His words angered her.

"Olive, don't you see? That's how I would feel moving to Kansas City. Just like one of those treasured but forgotten things. Waiting, and out of my element. Useless, and serving no purpose." With some effort, he stood up, signaling the end of their conversation. Finally he added, "Let's talk some more tomorrow. I'm all tuckered out."

Olive pictured herself jumping to her feet and shouting at him that this was not okay, that he had to start being realistic, to think about all the things that could go wrong here, that she was offering him a comfortable, easy life. But then she pictured the disbelief that would cloud his thoughtful face at her harshness and waved away the image. She had never spoken to him like that. Olive thought he looked weary, but strong, like he had always been. It was hard to think of him as old. Turning to fix her gaze on the fire in the fireplace, she said quietly, "Okay. Fair enough. Good night, Grandpa."

"Good night, Olive."

She watched him leave with Scout trotting dutifully behind him. Maybe he would be more reasonable in the morning after a good night's sleep, she thought. She felt discouraged though, bothered by what she concluded was his stubbornness. That was it. He was stubborn and set in his ways. He didn't know what was best for him. He just wasn't being practical. People become that way when they get older. Olive's annoyance grew. She was determined not to leave him alone at the cabin.

Before her mother died, she'd made Olive promise that she would look after her grandfather, but he was making it very difficult. He was just impossible. He had practically ignored her letters asking him to consider coming to live with her. When they did talk about it, he would invariably change the subject or speak in riddles.

When she was a child, she'd always enjoyed his fables. He told his fables to explain things she couldn't understand. It was how she'd learned many lessons. But now, she had to be the adult, the responsible one. Olive remembered her mother's exact words. "Olive, your Grandpa is the wisest, kindest man alive. You make sure his days are comfortable and contented, that he has whatever he needs. He's always looked after us, you know. You must do this for me, Olive, you must promise." And Olive had promised.

Olive looked around her. Her mother's life had ended here in this cabin with her grandfather by her side. Oddly, the image of it didn't distress her because it was what her mother wanted, and in her heart, Olive believed it was a good place to live and to die. She stood up, walked to the front window and looked out into the blackness of night.

The wind still raged. She could see that the moon was beginning to rise above the lake, creating a choppy path of white light in the water. The light was just enough that she could see the waves slam into shore, one after another after another. Each wave was different from the one before it. She was mesmerized by the rhythmic repetitiveness of it. It's like all of us, she thought, we come and go, leaving our inscription on the stones of the earth. That's all the permanence we get, really. Life goes on. Fleeting and predictable.

She placed another log on the fire. It rolled to the back of the fireplace, creating a brief crash and spark, blue flames licking it uncertainly. She watched this wondering how it was that her grandfather managed to ride his bike to town, stack firewood, read seven books a week, and thrive on so much reclusion. He did thrive in a way. He still had his glow and was as sharp as ever. But, no, she knew he couldn't stay here. What about the promise she had made to her mother? Besides, it just didn't make sense. He was old and moved slowly, slept more soundly. It's what people do when they get older; they move to safer places where someone can look after them.

Olive was restless. It would be impossible to sleep. The clock on the mantle ticked loudly. She began to pace without realizing it. Her pacing led into her grandfather's study. It was a small room, but cozy and inviting. She switched on the light and began to look through his collection of books. History, psychology, nature, novels, every topic imaginable was here.

Her eyes searched the rest of the room. The massive bookshelves, file cabinets, and stacks of periodicals made the little room appear vital, almost as though it had its own pulse. Maybe there was something here, just one thing, that would serve as evidence to her that he really was declining. Then she would be able to gently persuade him with a specific reason why he should return with her to Kansas. It would be that simple.

On his desk sat his old manual Royal typewriter, which he loved dearly. She smiled, thinking of him pounding out letters to congressmen, newspaper editors, and family on this obsolete thing. It was in immaculate shape, almost as though he'd polished it regularly. Behind the typewriter was a small cardboard box labeled "pencils—red, blue and #2B" and next to it a smaller box that contained several pink, white, and gray erasers.

Stacked in front of the boxes were three wooden rulers, a brass letter opener, and a large magnifying glass. Olive noticed that her grandfather had inscribed his initials on the rulers. Beside the three rulers were two field guidebooks for identifying northwestern songbirds. The books were earmarked with so many small scribbled notes that she wondered how he was ever able to successfully turn the pages.

Beneath the books, there was a folder filled with newspaper clippings. All of the clippings pertained to either local or national politics. He had written comments in red pencil on some of the clippings, as if he'd intended to write letters to the editor. Most of his comments were dated.

Under this folder was another folder he'd entitled "Erasable Bond," which contained a small stack of slightly yellowed typing paper. Still another folder held short grocery lists and partially completed letters he'd composed. The grocery lists were all similar: apples, pumpernickel bread, powdered milk, plum jelly, green beans, saltine crackers, and peppermints. The letters appeared to be to no one in particular. Most were written in pencil, and behind them were little sketches of birds and geese. Although the pencil was smudged in spots, Olive marveled at how detailed the sketches were.

At the bottom of the stack of books and folders, she noticed a package. It was some sort of book wrapped in oilcloth and tied with a piece of twine. Was it an intended gift? He had obviously taken great care in wrapping it, although the oilcloth looked worn. Very worn.

Olive decided it was not a gift. Slowly, she began to unwrap it. Halfway through, she stopped, feeling intrusive. She listened to the silence around her.

Overcome with the weight of responsibility she felt for her grandfather and Lottie, Olive sat down, pulling the chair close to the desk. Minutes passed as she listened to the ticking clock on the mantle. She hugged the oilcloth package to her as though it were a small breathing thing.

Eventually she placed the package on the desk and opened it tentatively, smoothing the oilcloth flat. It was a book. A sketchbook. No, a journal, some sort of journal. She began to thumb through it. There was an unsealed envelop just inside the journal's pages. It was not addressed to her, but to Lottie.

For a moment she just stared at it. She examined it, then placed it back inside the journal exactly as she had found it. She wrapped the journal back in the oilcloth and tied the twine. So it had been intended as a gift after all, she thought. And yet, it appeared to have been wrapped quite some time ago. Had he forgotten to give it to Lottie? Was it supposed to be a secret? But why? And what sort of book would he have wrapped so long ago? Lottie was barely eight years old.

Olive closed her eyes, inhaled deeply, then reached again for the package. She took a deep breath, then reached for the letter, opened it, and began to read.

My Dear Great Granddaughter Lottie,

Some rainy day, I hope you will find this letter and read it. I am very proud of what a bright young lady you have become. You have been a big help to your Aunt Olive and to me as well. Your mother and dad would be very proud of you. They loved you very much.

Someday, Lottie, your great Grandpa will not be here anymore. It's not a sad thing really, just the natural order of everything. I do wish I could tell you about what I have learned about life over the years on this land, which will someday belong to you. Truly, I've discovered a world I'd never imagined in my earlier years, which were spent obtaining degrees and titles.

There is a timeless wisdom that awaits you here unlike any other. You only need to be willing to listen and to see, to really see, what is around you. To be sensitive to nature, respect every creature, every puffy cloud, every breeze that blows, every tree that sways, and every frog that croaks.

Olive tells me you like to read, so I have written a story for you to read someday after I am gone. Perhaps this story will inspire you in some way to walk a gentle path through these north woods. And when you see your reflection in the lake, you will know you have not intruded. You will know that you belong.

Love,
Great Grandpa

Olive carefully folded the letter and tucked it back in the envelop. She opened the journal to the first page, placing the letter there. The first page appeared to be the beginning of a neatly typed story titled *The Legend of Blue Water Stones*. She smiled, remembering how her grandfather's stories had always been so imaginative. Sometimes the stories were full of adventure and other times full of comfort. She remembered sitting spellbound beside him when she was a young girl while he spun inventive tales that seemed to be just for her. He could make the most commonplace things enchanting.

Perhaps he knew he would not have enough time left in his life to do the same for Lottie. She thought about his letter. Lotttie was too young to truly understand the words, but she adored her great grandfather so much that she would have tried to understand. She would have tried to do exactly as he had said. Lottie would have willed herself to listen, to see, to appreciate every tiny thing, to walk a gentle path through the north woods.

Olive sighed. She pushed the chair back from the desk and resumed her pacing. There was no hope for sleep. The clock on mantle chimed quietly, then resumed ticking. The fire had died down to popping embers. She walked slowly to the kitchen and fixed a mug of steaming hot cocoa. While she sipped on the sweet chocolate, she gazed at her grandfather's empty rocking chair by the fireplace. For a moment she imagined him never again sitting there in its tapestry upholstered softness and wide wooden arms. She took a sharp breath.

Returning to his desk, she picked up the story meant for Lottie. She hesitated, setting it carefully back on the desk, patting the pages into place. Tentatively, she picked it up again. Reading a few pages would help lull her to sleep, she thought. She felt in need of a bit of comfort anyway.

Olive walked back to her grandfather's rocking chair, balancing the hot cocoa mug in her other hand. She lowered herself into the chair, sinking into the rocker's cushions, covering herself with a soft puffy quilt. Immediately she felt small, but safe. Very safe. She closed her eyes for a moment, then opening them wide began to read.

✏️❏ For my great granddaughter Lottie,
from Grandpa

The Legend of the Blue Water Stones

My dearest Lottie, one day when you travel
far, far to the north, past gray fields of slumbering
farmlands, you will discover a most magical place
where the earth turns blue when it meets the sky.
You will see brilliant blue pouring gently from the
horizon onto open land, creating a beautiful and
mysterious lake. From the heart of the lake, soft
breezes form waves that continually wash blue
onto a stone-covered beach, causing the stones to
be more richly colorful than any other known to
the world.

It will be clear to you that these are not ordinary
stones. There is something very curious about
them and something unexplainable about this
place. There is something strange in the way the
old cottonwood trees bend so easily to touch the
blue water. And something stranger still is the
way the birds, animals, and other creatures cling
to it. Almost no one knows the origin of the unusual
stones. Almost no one knows this, the true legend
of the Blue Water Stones...

You see, very few know that the blue water
stones came to be along the lakeshore ages ago at
the time when the moon broke free from Mother
Earth to dangle in the darkest night sky. In the
very instant that the young moon was alone, legend
tells us that he became filled with a loneliness
bigger than the whole universe. He could not yet
understand his importance to the earth. Nor did
he know anything about the rising and setting
sun.

At first, the young moon stayed in the sky too long at dawn while the sun rose, just so he could be a part of the light. He became distraught when the great sun, who colored the sky with pinks and lavenders, chased him away into the darkness.

"Who goes there?" exclaimed the sun in a booming voice, as the sky became lighter and lighter.

"It is me, the moon. I am from Earth, and I don't know what I'm to do!" the moon answered quietly. "I'm not used to such darkness."

"Well, Moon from Earth, you cannot stay here. There is only room enough for me and a few clouds in this sky. You must go and find your own way. Look for the North Star, she can help you. But you must leave now! We cannot both be here. Now, go! I must get back to work!"

So the moon sadly went in search of the North Star. And long before he discovered her and his new and dear friends the stars, even before he learned how bright he could shine in the night, he shed great solid tears of misery that fell to the earth.

His tears plunged to the small northern lakeshore, forming stones that scattered all along the blue water's edge. As each teardrop touched the ground, it became a new stone, taking on warmth and color and substance and character.

The moon blinked in astonishment as he gazed down at Earth and saw that his tears had acquired finely sculpted features, each one different from the next. They were like tiny planets, and when he looked hard enough he could see that they had big expressive faces with almost no bodies except for rounded bellies and knobby feet. Every one of them could close their eyes, become perfectly still and then ever so quietly retreat into themselves so that they looked as ordinary as any other common stone of the world. That was what would keep them safe. Henceforth, they would be the guardians of the sparkling blue water.

Anyone coming to the lake would have to pass over the stones. It was quite clear they were not adapted for travel, but then, there was no reason for them to ever leave the blue water shores.

As he marveled at the stones looking up at him in the night, the sky around him became a little brighter. And just then, the moon heard a soft voice call, "Do you see? Your teardrop stones will stay beside the blue water as a reminder to you that despite your earlier sadness, there will always be good things that follow. And from this time on, for those who have eyes to see and the hearts to follow, the stones will share secrets of long life. Now, come along, let me show you the night sky."

And at that very moment he knew. The young moon of Earth had found the North Star. He looked back one more time at the blue water stones.

- 2 -

WHISPERLEAF

Now, even in this age, you will see that high above the blue water's shore, along the bank, old cottonwood trees still watch over the stones night and day. One of the eldest of all the cottonwood trees was called Whisperleaf because she spoke so softly that she could barely be heard above the unceasing waves. The harsh winds of winter had twisted her trunk so close to the shore that she could gently touch the blue water stones when the breezes were just right.

She knew each stone by name. The moon's teardrop stones were her friends. Whisperleaf knew these stones were far more ancient and far wiser than she was. She had learned many things of great importance from them. Even in times of great bleakness, they'd told her, "Whisperleaf... look for the good...you must try to look for the good."

When she was young, and winters were long and sharp with ice, or summers were hot and waterless, she did not know what they meant. But as her trunk began to bend with age and she saw the timeless moon come and go, she began to realize what it was to look for the good.

Even so, Whisperleaf could not forget that day long ago when one of the stones was taken away from the lakeshore by a human child. The stone was called OldSkogmo, and he was the only stone Whisperleaf could ever remember actually leaving the blue water shores. She was a very young tree then, and it made her sad. And yet the other stones assured her that OldSkogmo would return someday with tales of other lands, and it would be good.

But to Whisperleaf, he was just gone. He had been her closest friend. She would never forget his kind and knowing face, his orange and black specked roundness, and the secrets of other times he shared with her. He had told her of the times before humans came when the cottonwoods were tall and plentiful. Yes, she missed that. Sometimes she wondered if he had somehow returned to the moon. She was very old now, and he had never come back.

And now, it was spring once again. All of them had survived another winter, and on this day Whisperleaf took courage in the early dawn's yellow sun rising up and over the woods behind her. She watched as a white-tailed deer arrived for a drink of the blue water. The young deer stepped lightly along the shore, never disturbing a thing. She was always extra careful when crossing over the little seashells.

Whisperleaf noticed a blue heron wading in the shallow water. As usual, the heron was stern and silent, like a statue, and seemed to be admiring his own reflection in the lake. At times he would bend his neck towards her and lift his giant wings for no apparent reason. Then suddenly, just as he had done so many times before, he lifted himself out of the water, gliding silently away to some secret place. Whisperleaf knew he would return to the same spot that evening as though he had never left.

As she watched the heron fly away, a giant Canadian goose landed noisily in the water. Two more geese landed after him. The first goose created a hubbub and was loud when he came to the blue water. He blurted out all his thoughts despite the stones' reminders that many things are better left unsaid. The goose tried hard to learn from the stones. He listened to all he was told and was better for it, but he still managed to be cumbersome and silly.

And yet, thought Whisperleaf, when the three huge geese returned to the sky, they were amazingly graceful, as though flight was the most effortless thing in the world.

Whisperleaf was gazing upward at the geese as they glided above the lake in a miniature V formation when there was a sudden crash and fluttering in her upper branches.

"Cau,,,cau…cau…caution! A storm, a dangerous storm…look to the north….cau… cau... caution!" screeched a large black crow who had landed heavily on her branch. Then all of a sudden he was gone. And there was nothing more. Only the bright chill of a spring morning.

It was so calm, yet Solosong, the black crow, was never wrong. As the day unfolded, darkness overtook the skies. A biting north wind began to whip through Whisperleaf's leaves. The deer lifted her head, alert, motionless, water dripping from the corners of her mouth, alarmed by the sudden change in the air. Then suddenly she bounded into the woods without a glance back. She did not see the lazy lapping waves turn into crashing white-caps slamming into the stones.

The wind whirled around faster and faster, lifting bits of sand and small shells off the shore. The stones began one by one to close their eyes and retreat into themselves.

Whisperleaf braced herself against the onslaught of icy rain. Her new spring leaves were twisted, torn, and blown away. The sky became darker, the wind even stronger. She felt her trunk bend to the point of almost breaking. The smaller cottonwoods shivered and tried to resist, only to be tossed around like twigs. Stabbing ice pellets mixed with snow, frozen clouds dropped to the earth and swirled into drifts of white on the ground.

The wind became a green black hissing beast devouring everything in its path. Lake debris swirled through the air. Immense cracking sounds overtook the screaming wind. It became colder and colder as if winter had returned in a savage fury against spring. The wind raged on, spitting ice, which turned to sleet, then sheets of endless rain. The sky seemed to roar with gray water rolling out of black clouds.

Then there was just rain. Somewhere in the distance, Whisperleaf thought she heard the black crow calling, but the downpour drowned out the sound. The wind had stopped. After a long while, the rain became a pitter-patter sound and a streak of pink light appeared in the western sky. It was over. Only then did Whisperleaf realize that one of her largest branches had been partially ripped and was hanging close to the ground.

"Whisperleaf?" Large round eyes were fixed on her. It was Skeedad who spoke. He was a portly black stone with bold orange stripes outlining his perfectly sculpted face. He had a spiral of narrow stripes wrapped around his belly and stubby feet planted firmly in the sand. A small wave washed over him. His tiny nose wrinkled slightly as he gazed up at her. He frowned thoughtfully, then smiled. His smile was nearly as big as his face. "Are you alright?"

Whisperleaf saw that he was filled with curiosity and warmth, causing her to forget the storm and answer, "Why, yes, of course, except for this branch…"

Skeedad tottered closer to her on his knobby feet. He tumbled forward, then righted himself. Looking up, he surveyed the injured branch, blinked his giant eyes at her and sighed, "Ah, yes…I can hear you better now…look how very close you are to us."

She had not realized this and just as she began to marvel at their closeness, the giant Canadian goose and his two friends landed in the lake with a great splash, causing Skeedad to roll backward into the shallow water.

"Gaak! How ghastly, how hideous! Look at that ugly branch! And look how your leaves are torn away! Whisperleaf, the storm has absolutely ravaged you to bits. Gaak, how horrid! How very hid—"exclaimed the goose who stopped himself immediately when he saw the stones turn scornful eyes to him, just as Skeedad was rolling himself back onto the sand.

"Um...yes...well, it was a fierce storm and you survived it quite well enough, good Whisperleaf," the second goose said. The third goose, stood tall and flapped his great wings in agreement, while the first goose looked shamefully at the ground.

"How very excellent it will be to have your shade in the heat of summer. Don't you think so, too, Silverdew?" Skeedad asked, casting a warning glance at the first goose. A tiny droplet of water trickled down Skeedad's face.

Whisperleaf considered Skeedad's words and did not mention that she felt a bit weaker and older.

In the days and weeks that followed, spring turned slowly to summer. There was real warmth from the sun. The sky became a powdery blue with friendly clouds dancing here and there. The white-tailed deer and the blue heron came each dawn and each sunset, and the three geese spent whole days wandering lazily along the shore. Skeedad and the other stones traded tales of other springs and summers and absorbed the goodness of each day with Whisperleaf close by. Her tender spring leaves were full now. Even the ripped branch had shiny leaves that touched the damp sand.

Once on a clear and peaceful night, when the moon was full and reflected on the water, one of the youngest cottonwoods asked Whisperleaf, "What are we to fear, Whisperleaf?"

"Should we fear storms?" another asked.

"And, will there be other dangers?" a very tiny cottonwood asked.

"Storms are not to be feared. Yes, some are very powerful but the black crow, Solosong, lets us know before they are upon us so we are ready. It is just the way of nature. Humans are another thing altogether. You cannot ever be ready for humans. They are to be feared because you cannot know what they might do," Whisperleaf said in her quiet careful way.

"Yes, and although that is true, there are humans who are good and would not harm us," Skeedad said. "Once long, long ago before Whisperleaf's time, when the cottonwoods were tall and plentiful, there were humans who came here at the break of every day. As they aged, their footsteps became shaky and slow. Sometimes they would sit in complete silence under the cottonwoods. Their skin had lines deeper than bark and their hair was the color of a moonless night. They never caused us any harm."

"I remember them well," a smaller red stone said. She had an earnest face with big inquisitive eyes, a rounded nose and mouth. She looked upward when she spoke as though she was snatching words right out of the sky. Her red color, unusual for a blue water stone, was speckled all over with white and black dots, which made her glitter even in the earliest moonlight.

"They wore feathers in their hair and their steps were light as any deer," the red stone continued, looking at each tiny cottonwood. "They came here from the water in a little boat made of trees."

At the mention of trees, the young cottonwoods began to whisper to each other. They seemed worried.

"A boat made of trees?" one of them finally asked.

"Yes, but the trees' spirits had already gone to be above the sky," she answered. Sensing their relief, she continued, "There were other humans, too, at that time, but they stayed away because they believed rival spirits danced on the shores of this land."

"Which, in fact, is true," Skeedad said. Skeedad knew all about spirits. He had an ability to perceive all the ghosts that had ever been along the blue water shores.

"Those humans were very courageous, indeed," the small red stone concluded. Skeedad nodded in agreement, momentarily tipping too far forward, his face touching the beach.

"And, there was one human who came here alone many moon seasons later. We called him Brookdweller. You remember him," a plain orange stone said looking from Whisperleaf to Skeedad.

The orange stone had an elongated face with large droopy eyes under an angular brow that made him appear to be frowning all the time. He was larger than the other stones and a bit clumsy. Because of his odd shape, he had to lean slightly against the small red stone to keep from teetering forward. Despite his gawky appearance, they listened to him intently because he was always able to recall any detail of any time and jog their memory of it. He'd once told them that he could even remember as far back as when he had been a tear falling from the moon.

"He built his house over there beyond the grassy bank at the edge of the woods without disturbing the land. Very uncommon for a human," he said. Whisperleaf followed his gaze towards the bank and waved her upper branches slightly.

"Yes, yes, we remember Brookdweller," the stones replied in unison.

"Brookdweller's spirit will always be here," Skeedad said. "He was kind and gentle. He loved the earth and respected every creature, a rare quality for a human. He understood about the order of creation."

Whisperleaf knew this had always been important to Skeedad. She felt the same way. Creatures needed to be respected for who they were. It was only right.

She swayed a little in the evening breeze, remembering Brookdweller. The first time she saw him, he was a young man. He wandered so frequently along the lakeshore to and from the little brook, and he became known as Brookdweller. Every day he walked in the same direction the heron had flown in the morning. It was as though he might be searching for the heron. And yet, Brookdweller kept a respectful distance from creatures who might be wary of him. He seemed to know he was a stranger to this place.

"Brookdweller would take a blue water stone in his hand and turn it over and over, studying the stone as if he were searching for something," Skeedad said. "Many nights he would stand at the water's edge, gazing up at the moon. He spoke no words. Then, at times, he would speak directly to the stones as though he actually saw us. Yes. actually saw us for who we are! How could that be, with our eyes closed and looking like any other common stone of the world?"

Skeedad closed his eyes for a moment, then opened them wide and added, "It was quite odd, of course, but not frightening and certainly not a danger. He's been gone a long time now, but we have not forgotten him."

"Not forgotten him...not a danger," several of the stones repeated quietly.

Skeedad looked at the young cottonwoods with great fondness and said, "Humans are not always to be feared. Just be cautious and be prepared for the unpredictable."

"Be prepared for the unpredictable," Whisperleaf murmured.

The young cottonwoods gazed appreciatively at her and bowed slightly.

"Be prepared for the unpredictable..." they whispered.

"Be cautious," the small red stone added, looking upward at the night's first twinkling stars. She watched the enormous yellow moon rise above the lake into the black velvet sky. It created a path of warm light in the dark water.

All of them followed her gaze and felt sheltered in the moon's light.

"Be cautious, be prepared....and always remember to look for the good," Skeedad concluded thoughtfully.

And so it went. There were other stories of times gone by told by the stones. As days grew longer, the sunsets became more orange and the warmth of each day stayed with them into the night. Whisperleaf considered all they spoke of and wondered what had become of OldSkogmo who told the best tales of all.

In fact, Whisperleaf was beginning to wonder where the black crow Solosong had gone. It was not like him to be away for so long. She had not heard his voice since the strong storm of spring, which had torn her branch. She mentioned his absence to the stones, but they seemed unconcerned. They never fretted about things like that. Time moved differently for them.

© C. J. Clark

- 3 -

SOLOSONG

 The small black crow gazed at the moonlit lake from where he was perched in an old pine tree. The water was so still, it could have been ice. Even the slightest ripple could be heard. Owls hooted into the darkness and night animals scurried through underbrush. There was a plodding sound of deer hooves following narrow trails though the woods to the lake, then pounding away after a cool drink of water. The sound seemed to go on forever. Far in the distance there was the yip and howl of a coyote's song blended into melody. Then silence. The quiet was like a vast space not yet filled. For the small crow it was not like any other night. He waited. He knew how to wait.

When dawn finally arrived in the eastern sky, the little crow stretched his wings to greet the new day. All was well on North Point. All was well and yet as the sun began to warm the sky, he began to practice his warning call, "Cau…Cau…Cau…!"

He kept this up for a time until the morning was filled with twittering songbirds. The raucous call of a blue heron and the laugh of a loon resounded across the lake. A formation of Canadian geese appeared in the sky above him. The geese seemed to fill the entire sky. Their honking sounds were deafening. His call was lost, and he fell silent.

He soared upward, then down, following the tree line along the lake and landing in a young birch tree. This caught the attention of the creatures along the shore which pleased him. Since he had nothing to warn them about, he flew away, returning to the old pine tree, last night's haven. All was well on North Point. He dozed.

Suddenly he was seized with panic as a dark shadow fell over him. Startled, he looked up only to be blinded by the sun. He looked down and saw it again. A looming darkness on the land seemed to grow into a giant shape. There was a crash in the branch beside him.

"All is well on North Point?" It was Solosong from Stony Point. He had returned as promised. The younger crow was in complete awe of the large older crow and was unable to utter a sound. Solosong seemed to understand the silence. He waited.

It was Solosong's patience that made it possible for this young crow to learn his duties. Solosong had patrolled North Point and Stony Point all spring and early summer since the Elder CauSong of North Point had gone to live above the sky. Long, long ago, Elder CauSong had taught Solosong the ways of the lake creatures and what he must do as an honorable crow to alert them to danger.

And now, here was this young crow, willing to learn the ways. It was not a usual life for a crow, but the little crow was bright and capable of carrying on the path of Elder CauSong. Solosong was sure of this. It was already summer and little crow had spent his first day and night alone. It had gone well. He was ready. Solosong could return to Stony Point.

"Solosong, there are some things I still need to know," the young crow began tentatively.

Solosong looked ahead, scanning the horizon for anything different. He waited for the young crow to finish.

"How long am I to stay with the lake creatures after I have sounded the warning alarm?" He wasn't sure, and it seemed important.

Solosong turned to look at the smaller crow and said, "You do not stay...you alert them to what is coming and then you go. You fly away. When the trouble has passed, you alert them from where you have taken cover. They will hear you. You are a crow. It is your song. It is unlike any other."

Together they listened to the sounds of the day, the lake breeze rustling through leaves, the steady slapping sound of waves on stones, a wood-pecker hammering a hollow tree. There were sounds of finches flitting about, of chattering chip-munks, and the sweep of pine needles against the breeze.

Solosong knew that the young crow would follow a solitary path all his days. He watched a small white cloud drift by and said nothing more for a time.

Finally the little crow interrupted the silence. "What will they call me, Solosong?"

"Lonesong of North Point," Solosong said thoughtfully.

Lonesong puffed himself up as large as he could and settled into the name. It was good.

"Of all the lake creatures," Solosong said, "the Blue Water Stones will always tell you what you need to know. They have been here the longest, even here on this North Point. Their wisdom comes from an endless time of absorbing the goodness of spirits that have gone on and from being intense observers. They will teach you how to look for the good. You will come to understand if you just listen to the stones." With this, he soared upward and was gone.

Solosong dipped and soared and sliced through clouds and deep blue sky, believing himself to be an eagle or a hawk. He called into the air as loud as he could, his voice lost in the wind. He flew towards the sun, the warm summer sun. It was red and low in the sky. He soared upwards over treetops and creeks of babbling water. Onward he flew, hurled through space as though he were just one feather, light and swift.

Finally he landed in a stand of poplars where he heard the sound of another crow calling.

"All is well on the West Point?" Solosong bellowed.

"All is well. You are returning to Stony Point, Solosong?" the calling crow asked.

"Yes. It is time. The sun is warm. The North Point is at peace." Barely did he finish the words when he shot up and away and on to Stony Point. It was nearly nightfall.

When he returned to Stony Point, he landed with unusual softness in the upper branches of his friend, Whisperleaf. He made no sound. He could see that Whisperleaf had been damaged by the last violent storm of winter, and he felt sad. Still, he said nothing. The stones, shells, and cottonwoods, the white-tailed deer, the blue heron, and even the three silly geese looked up at him in anticipation. But he had no warning alarm for them this time. The stones were the first to understand this.

"Welcome back, Solosong." Skeedad was always the first to speak.

Making no reply, Solosong launched himself upward with all the grace he could muster. He glided above the shore, turned sharply, and flew higher, above the trees, the ironwoods, the elms, the pines, and spruce trees. He continued on until there was just open meadow below him. Then he turned once more, back toward the lakeshore where he stopped a fair distance away, settling in a giant maple. All was well on Stony Point.

From his perch in the maple tree, he could hear the stones telling tales of ages ago when there were large fierce animals that came to the lakeshore to drink. Even the peaceful animals needed a loud crow to warn them of the presence of such beasts so they could flee the danger. The white-tailed deer had never had to fear those animals. They had long since gone to be above the sky. Skeedad spoke of them with great fondness and seemed to miss them, although there had been many crow lifetimes since then.

Solosong was certain that the fierce animals had been replaced by humans. Skeedad probably knew this, too, but it was said that he did not speak often of humans after OldSkogmo had been taken away by the child.

Skeedad spoke of ice storms and winter blizzards that covered their entire world in slumber. The stones would withdraw into their own warmth and the only trees still green and watching were the pine, fir and spruce.

One quiet summer morning, Solosong awoke from his rest with an overpowering feeling of sheer dread. He looked to the skies and saw nothing unusual. There was nothing strange in the south breeze. He could see that the stones, Whisperleaf, and all the creatures were content in their places. Still, he felt a sense of darkness that would not go away. It stayed with him throughout the day.

As he became increasingly nervous, he decided to fly to the North Point by the longest route. This meant he would travel above fields and great open meadows south before switching back north. It just seemed right. He didn't know why. It did not matter why. He was never wrong about his feelings of danger.

With a quick glance back at Stony Point, he set off on his journey. He flew higher and further than he ever did this time of year. There were cheery puffs of white clouds hanging low in the sky that greeted him along the way. Southward he flew, over a small town and over farms with enormous fields of young corn, cows plodding through pastures, solitary human dwellings, tiny lakes, and pine woods. The wind was warm and strong. Solosong saw everything. And yet there was nothing of danger. It was just the feeling of something not right.

He circled back to the north, hovering, soaring, darting to the east, then west. He lingered in the sky, watching.

Then he saw it. There was no mistaking the slow methodical movement of a car on the road below. It was a big shiny intrusion. It stirred the gravel road into great clouds of brown dust. It was loud. And it was ugly against the landscape. Humans, he thought.

The car traveled past the pines, the tiny lakes, the small dwellings, the cows, the fields of corn, and was almost to the small town when Solosong, sure of its path, flew fast like a bullet taking the crow's route back to Stony Point.

As he streaked across the sky, the wind zipping through his wings, stinging him with fatigue, he thought he remembered Skeedad saying, "...not all humans are to be feared." Still, he had to warn them. "Just be cautious," Skylo, the red stone, had said.

So he flew with every bit of strength he had, thinking only of his friends Whisperleaf, the stones, the sea shells, the white-tailed deer, the heron, and the geese. He thought of their world, peaceful and good. The storm was one thing, humans were something else. It was his duty to warn them. He was Solosong of Stony Point.

When he spotted Whisperleaf, he landed this time with a crash and screech, darting from uppermost branch to branch, screaming, "Cau...Cau.. Caution!"

"What is it, Solosong?" Skeedad asked, alert, curious.

"Solosong?" Whisperleaf was shaken.

"Humans coming from the south. Cau... Cau...Caution!"

Solosong repeated the alarm just once until he could feel all the lake creatures become tense and wary. It was all he could do. He was exhausted. His task was complete. He shot upward and was gone.

© C.J. Clark

- 4 -
goodScout

One more turn to go and they would be there. The big yellow dog pressed her nose against the window and whined until it was opened for her. Crisp northern air rushed in and filled the car. It was cool and vaguely familiar to the dog. As the car rounded the last corner and made its way down the hill, the strong scent of rain-washed woods filled her nostrils. There it was. The lake. Yes. She could see it now. She almost leapt out of the car window. There was a crow's loud cawing, and looking up, she spotted three geese climbing higher into the blue sky. She was almost certain she had been here before. Yes, she was sure she had.

As the car pulled into the narrow drive, the sun was setting in an explosion of bright colors reflected perfectly in the lake. The door nearest the dog opened and she streaked out, barely touching the ground. Splash! She was shoulder deep in the cool blue water.

"Wait for me! Wait!"

A brown-haired child raced after the dog, picked up a small branch and hurled it into the water. She ripped her sneakers off, tossed them onto the bank, and pushing stray curls off her face, she rolled up her jeans. Timidly, she stepped into the lake just as a frothy wave washed over her toes. The water was so cold, she shivered a little.

"Go, go get the stick, go on—it's over there!" she squealed.

The big yellow dog splashed happily through the shallow water, pretending to search for the clumsily thrown branch. The child bounded into the water after her yelling, "No, look! See? It's there! Over there!"

The dog swam toward the branch, snatched it out of the water, and brought it to the child.

"You found it! Good Scout! Good dog!" The child was drenched and laughing. The dog adored this game.

Scout charged up the bank and rolled onto her back in the tall grass. Panting, she gazed up at the cloudless dusky sky, then suddenly sprung to her feet and dashed back to the lake. Dipping her nose into the clear blue water, she took a drink. The water was cool and refreshing, not like anything she had tasted before.

A woman's voice sounded from the cabin. "Don't let Scout go in the water. It's almost time to come inside."

Well, it was too late for that. The girl and the dog continued frolicking in and out of the water until the sun dipped out of sight. Then out came the big towel, and Scout had to endure being dried off for what seemed like forever.

"Good, Scout. C'mon, let's go in before we get in trouble."

But the dog did not follow. Instead she stopped and tuned her senses to everything around her. Somewhere in the distance she could hear the eerie laugh of a loon calling from the liquid darkness of the lake. The sound hung there in the stillness of the new nightfall.

Then there was that other sound. Not a dog. It was more like a howl, no, a yip, but not familiar to her. It was hypnotic. She took a few steps away from the cabin into the dark. An owl hooted in the tree above her. It startled her, and she jumped backward, overturning a bucket. The bucket made an unbearably loud clanking sound that broke the stillness. From the lakeshore, a deer bounded past her, crashing through underbrush into the depths of the woods.

Then it was quiet. Looking back at the lake, Scout was puzzled to see the huge old cottonwood tree sway slightly, although there was no breeze or anything to cause it to move like that. Just as she was about to investigate, she heard her name called.

"Scout! Where are you?" It was the woman looking for her in the first bit of moonlight. The moon was bright and full, creating a large path of white light on the water.

Starting towards the woman, Scout thought she heard tiny voices coming from the lake. She froze with uncertainty. She barked, just once. It was a dull and flat sound that did not belong here. An immediate hush fell over the lake. The little voices vanished.

"There you are! C'mon Scout, what are you doing out here?"

This time Scout followed along. Inside the cabin she found a fleece dog bed by the fireplace where a friendly crackling fire warmed the cabin. Suddenly overwhelmed with weariness, she curled up and slept.

Early the next morning, Scout awoke to the sound of geese honking. Rising from her comfy bed, she stretched, trotted to the window, and looked out. Three Canadian geese had landed in the water where she'd played the evening before. They were massive creatures. She had a vague recollection of chasing geese like these far into the sky when she was just a puppy. It had been a ridiculous game. There had been a whole flock of them and they had waited until she was right up on them, when suddenly, with a massive flapping of wings, all of them took off at once, honking loud protests all the way. The rush of wing beats was staggering. And there she was, left alone on land, with nothing but her own shadow.

She watched the three geese as they swam in the shallow water close to the cabin. They glided leisurely, creating long ripples in the lake. The water was so still, like liquid glass, reflecting the lavender morning. One of the geese waddled up on to the shore and lingered by the old cotton-wood tree, making occasional loud cackling sounds. Scout watched the lakeshore activity from the window as she waited for the woman and child to awaken. At that moment, it seemed as though time did not move.

But eventually it did. Soon the woman and child were up and about starting their day. After the usual bustle of morning household activities, they pulled on hiking boots and grabbed Scout's leash as they headed for the door.

"Scout! Want to go for a walk?" the woman called. With a hasty pat on the big dog's head, a leash was snapped to her collar. The woman was dressed warmly in jeans and a flannel shirt with a baseball cap to shade her eyes. A small good-natured person, she looked ready for anything.

"Scout, we're walking to the creek," the child said. Her curly hair was pulled back away from her face, showing off big blue eyes and rosy cheeks. The red flannel shirt she wore was too large for her and likely belonged to the woman. It made her look tiny.

"Does she have to have this leash? Scout won't run away."

"She was just a puppy when she was here last, Lottie. She could get lost. Besides the woods by the creek is probably really overgrown. Who knows what we'll find! We'll have to blaze our own trail. Exciting, huh?" the woman said, laughing lightly.

The creek, thought Scout, now that was something. It was all coming back to her even though she had been such a pup last time. The creek held all sorts of wonders. Leading to it they found narrow paths made by deer and other smaller animals. The trees grew thick, making it almost impassible. The creek itself was shallow and clear as air. It curved and nestled itself between banks of tall trees with shimmering leaves. At one end there were cattails, so tall and dense that it was difficult to see where the creek met the lake.

Part of the creek tumbled over stones and reeds, forming a little brook of constantly moving water. It became wider and deeper as it moved further away from the brook, as though it gained power and purpose in its journey to the next lake.

Scout wanted to follow the creek, lake to lake, chasing the scents that enveloped her at every turn. She kept her nose to the earth, breathing in and memorizing all the unfamiliar smells.

"Look, Lottie, this is where Grandpa used to hike when he first came here," the woman said, pointing to a pile of stones that made a natural bridge across the brook to a huge old tree stump. It was a perfect sitting stump.

All of a sudden the child gasped. "Aunt Olive! Look!"

Scout, suddenly alert, jerked her head up in time to see a large blue heron glance sternly in their direction, then lift off like a slow plane out of the cattails. It had been so close, they could see the stark yellow of its eyes and feel the movement of air from its wing beats. It didn't occur to Scout to bark, or chase, or to do anything but stare in disbelief. It had been so close.

"Did you see that, Scout?" Lottie asked, as if the dog might answer.

Scout wagged her tail in response. What was it about that heron? Something odd and beckoning about that stern look. The heron knew something. Something important. She shook off the feeling and bounded ahead.

They took their time hiking back to the cabin. The path they took through the woods was so thick that the sun could only break through in tiny patches of dancing light. The earth was black and rich and had the strong aroma of decaying leaves.

They hiked through an open meadow towards the lake, which led them to a stony beach. Waves lapped over the shore, spraying a fine mist of lake water over the stones. They stepped carefully over slippery stones. Scout slowed her pace for the woman and child who kept stumbling over the larger stones, laughing and talking and hanging on to each other to keep from falling.

They just weren't paying attention to the same things the dog noticed. Didn't they see that there was something peculiar about the stones? Scout had an odd feeling. She sniffed at the stones. What was it? She heard a loud cawing sound close by. She looked up. The sound was persistent and unsettling. The woman and child didn't seem to be aware of it. They kept talking about how beautiful the stones were. Scout didn't find the stones beautiful. There was just something curious about them.

"What's that?" Lottie asked suddenly, hearing a new sound in the distance.

Scout cocked her head to one side, listening. There was a buzzing noise coming from the grassy bank in front of the cabin. It was becoming louder and louder as they approached.

"It sounds like…oh, no, surely not…!" Aunt Olive exclaimed, quickening her pace.

She tripped over a pile of larger stones, caught herself, then scrambled ahead in the direction of the sound. She was almost running.

"Mr. Peterson!" Aunt Olive shouted, waving her arms, trying to be heard over the buzzing saw. "What are you doing?"

The noise stopped. A lanky blonde man flashed a wide smile at her.

"Hello, Olive." He stood beside the old cottonwood with the saw running on low at his side. A few branches lay on the ground next to the tree. "Good to see you. When did you get up here?"

"Mr. Peterson, what are you doing?" Aunt Olive asked again, ignoring his greeting.

"Oh! Well, this tree. I figured you'd want it cut down soon. I was just getting a start on it. We had a bad storm early spring. High winds, ice, a lot of rain. This old cottonwood looks like it got beat up real bad in that spring storm. I could stack up some firewood for you." Hesitantly, he added, "Your grandfather always had me go ahead and take care of the trees."

"My grandfather. Well, you know Grandpa's not here anymore. It's just Lottie and me now, and I don't want you to touch that old tree."

"You must be joking. Look at it. It's so old. How many years could it have left anyway?" His voice trailed off as Lottie and Scout climbed onto the bank.

Scout trotted over to the tree and sat staring at Mr. Peterson. She considered growling at him, but he already looked uneasy.

"No. I'm not joking. Please. Maybe later." Aunt Olive didn't know why she felt so strongly about the old cottonwood at that moment. But as she looked from Scout to Lottie, she became strong in her resolve.

"Well…okay. It's your choice," Mr. Peterson said as he shrugged his shoulders. He ran his fingers through his blonde hair and gave her a friendly grin.

"Hope you folks have a good vacation. Let me know if you need anything." With that he walked off without looking back. They could hear him climb into his truck and drive away.

Aunt Olive looked back at Scout and Lottie. She really didn't know why she felt the way she did about the old tree. It was obvious that it might not live through too many more winters. Maybe she should have let Mr. Peterson cut it down.

Just as she began to doubt her decision, Scout jumped up and slapped her big paws onto the cottonwood, looking straight up into its branches, wagging her tail. The sight was so comical that she and Lottie began to laugh, forgetting about Mr. Peterson's visit.

The following weeks at the cabin were long and peaceful. Aunt Olive and Lottie took Scout with them everywhere they went. She went with them on their trips to town, trips in the boat, trips to visit old friends, and even trips to the county flea market. Mostly though, they stayed at Stony Point where each day was a new adventure. They were more relaxed than they had ever been.

It was the nights that made her uneasy. There was just too much activity outside the cabin after dark. The moon was brighter and more imposing than she had ever seen. On several occasions she heard those small hushed voices coming from the lakeshore. And the cottonwoods seemed to have an ability to rustle their leaves without the slightest breeze. When Scout tried to alert Aunt Olive and Lottie, they ignored her and told her to come inside.

Every dawn, without fail, a crow would call from the old cottonwood tree. It was that same persistent, disturbing call she'd heard before. It always followed that the three geese who were there at daybreak would fly away, not to be seen again until the next morning.

One evening, Lottie picked up an orange stone and tossed it into the shallow water. Immediately Scout felt compelled to retrieve the stone. She ran to it, dunked her head under the water and carefully scooped it up into her mouth, dropping it back on the lakeshore exactly where it had been.

Considering this to be an amazing feat, Lottie picked it up to throw again, but this time Scout caught it midair. She gently carried it in her mouth, then dropped it back on the shore again. Lottie lost interest in the game when Aunt Olive called her from the cabin.

As Lottie dashed away, Scout glanced back at the bright orange stone. It was large and angular, not particularly unusual. Just as she started to turn away, she thought she saw a little face looking back at her. She was startled to see that the stone had eyes, a tiny nose, and a mouth that formed a wide smile. And the little face was gazing steadily back at her with giant unblinking eyes. She shook her head in disbelief. A face? And it was looking right at her. How is that possible? When she looked again, the face was not there. The orange stone was nestled amongst the other stones just as it had been. Puzzled, she stood there for a long time, watching.

After that, she spent even more time by the water's edge, wandering this way and that, sniffing the breezes. Sometimes she would paw at the stones, turning them over trying to find the orange stone's face, but she never did.

She rested on the sand in the shade of the huge cottonwood, listening to the water wash over the stones. The cottonwood had a low lying branch that made a perfect hiding place. It was good that they'd not allowed Mr. Peterson to cut down the old tree.

Aunt Olive and Lottie began to spend more time on the lakeshore, too. Lottie made little castle-like structures out of the sand and collected stones and seashells in a small pail. When she wasn't looking, Scout would pick the stones and shells out of the pail one by one and deposit them back on the shore.

The woman and child splashed and swam in the lake and paddled the canoe a short distance into the water. Sometimes Scout would swim alongside the canoe, and they would cheer her on, as though it were a race and the dog was winning.

Late one afternoon, close to the end of their vacation, Lottie decided to take a walk with Scout, leaving Aunt Olive behind at the cabin. They were going to walk along the shore only a short distance. Aunt Olive told her not to go too far because it looked as though it might storm.

Off they went into the sunless afternoon, stepping over stones and wading in the shallow water where minnows nipped playfully at their toes. They charged together up onto the soft grass of the bank and paused there while Lottie fed cracked corn to the greedy chipmunks. Racing back to the shore, they chased and splashed and made a game of it all.

The wind began to blow in strong gusts, but they didn't notice it until Lottie's cap was blown straight up off her head. It flew away as though it had wings, and together they chased it along its flight path.

The cap was carried by the wind so far that they almost gave up running after it. By the time they did catch up to it, it had lodged in a tree deep in the woods, and Lottie had to climb up to retrieve it. Only then did they realize how dark the sky had become. It would be night soon and the oncoming storm made the daylight disappear faster. The sky turned from gray to dark blue to black. They started back towards the lakeshore when it began to sprinkle and then rain in a soft steady shower.

All at once Lottie stopped. Scout sat beside her searching the horizon. They had gone far. Somehow, they were all turned around and had lost their direction. The wind and rain and darkness made things worse.

"It's this way, Scout..." she said, turning the opposite direction. She began to walk faster, wiping rain water off her face. It was so dark. There was no moonlight to guide them, not a speck of any kind of light.

"No, wait, this can't be right." Now Lottie was frightened. She could not see ahead of her.

"Scout, can you find the way?"

Scout sniffed the air, but all the scents mixed together in the rain.

She pawed at the ground, digging up more scents but they were unfamiliar. Everything was beginning to smell like damp sand or wet wood. The wind howled just enough to bully the waves into whitecaps. In their fury to crash into shore, they drowned out any sounds familiar to Scout.

As it began to rain harder, they took cover under a huge fallen tree, but it was not much shelter. They were soaked, and Lottie began to shiver.

"We're lost, Scout," she whimpered, her voice carried away in the wind. She began to sob.

Scout licked the little girl's face and tried to comfort her, but she knew they had to move away from this spot and find their way back to the cabin. She listened. What was it? Something out there. There was a brief lull in the storm.

"GoodScout, over here, this is the way...come back this way...follow the shore..."

Startled, the big yellow dog stood up, her hair bristled with alarm. The voice was calling her from far away. Who was that? It was such an unusual voice, small, but strong and sure. She shook her head as though to clear the sound from her ears. Her tension and disbelief only served to scare Lottie, who crawled even further under the tree trunk.

"GoodScout…follow our voices, it's this way," another voice beckoned.

For some reason that she would not understand for a long, long time, Scout felt calm and certain of the path ahead. She nudged the child, who at first refused to budge until she sensed the dog's urgency. Lottie did not seem to hear the voices. She got up only at Scout's insistence.

Instantly, the two were blinded and drenched with sheets of rainwater. A tree limb snapped and crashed to the earth beside them. The darkness was like a black veil, and the wind tossed leaves and twigs around them in frantic swirls. Lottie took hold of Scout's collar but could barely keep up with the dog as she forged ahead.

"GoodScout…this way…not far…keep on…" said the voices, closer now. And the big yellow dog kept on, slogging through water, tripping over unseen obstacles, on and on she plodded. Every time she would open her eyes in an attempt to see ahead, rainwater would blind her. She just had to follow the voices.

"Go up on the bank, stay out of the water! This way! GoodScout, almost…" The dog and child climbed out of the water onto the bank just as thunder clapped and a lightening flash brightened the sky.

In the momentary light, Scout could see that they had narrowly escaped a deep drop off in the water. The pouring rain never let up as they continued trudging along the bank, losing their footing every few steps. The voices were closer and closer, and the dog moved faster and faster with Lottie hanging on to her collar.

"One more bend, follow the shore, goodScout."

Just then a small dot of light parted the rainwater and they heard Aunt Olive shouting, "Lottie! Scout!" as she shined a flashlight in their direction. She ran to them, snatching Lottie in her arms and hugging the dog at the same time.

"Lottie, I told you not to go far," she scolded.

"But my cap blew away...we had to chase it." Lottie whimpered, then began to laugh. She looked at the dog. "Scout brought us back. I don't know how she knew the way. We were really lost. It was so dark."

Together they hugged the dog, then trudged inside, shaking off water as they went. Scout paused at the door, looking back at the lakeshore. The voices were gone now. There was only the plink of raindrops on leaves, earth, and stones.

The next day was cool and bright. It would be autumn before long. Aunt Olive and Lottie began packing to return south, while Scout wandered on the beach. She sniffed and nudged the stones, searching for the little stone face she'd seen a few weeks before.

After a while, one of the stones held her interest more than the others because she caught a glimpse of it looking at her when she sat very, very still. It had a kindly face and did not seem at all afraid of her. It watched her intently. Did this stone help her find the way out of the storm? Did the voices she heard sometimes at night belong to the stones? It was just all so odd.

And why had they called her goodScout instead of Scout, which was the name given to her by humans. Even so, she felt protected and at ease here, and strangely she felt like she belonged.

From this time on, she would be goodScout, no matter what humans called her. After all, humans missed so many obvious things. She stretched her front legs so that the tips of her paws touched the water's edge just as a wave washed into shore. Lake mist lightly sprayed her face. She closed her eyes and shook briskly, her ears flapping over her head. Yes, it made perfect sense to her; she had become goodScout.

The old cottonwood's leaves brushed lightly against her face as if to confirm the kinship to the lakeshore. It would be time for the dog to leave soon.

"Scout, let's go!" Aunt Olive called.

Lottie appeared on the bank and called to her, "C'mon, Scout time to go in the car." But the dog didn't come to her.

Scout sniffed for one last moment at the kindly-faced stone .

"Aunt Olive, look at this beautiful stone Scout found," Lottie exclaimed, now standing beside the dog on the lakeshore. She reached for the black stone with the bold orange stripes.

Aunt Olive bent to look at the stone and agreed that it was very beautiful indeed and picked it up. Scout gently took the stone from her hand and deliberately dropped it back on the shore.

"Good, Scout. Do you like that stone?" asked Lottie, misunderstanding the dog's intent.

Aunt Olive picked it up again and this time Lottie took it from her saying, "Let's take it along. It's so pretty. Look how shiny and colorful it is."

And so, she carried the stone away from Stony Point with Scout close behind her. As they pulled away to leave, they could hear the loud cawing of a crow from a distant meadow.

©C.J. Clark

- 5 -

Deweye

The last thing he remembered was Whisperleaf telling him to look for the good. She didn't say final words like farewell or good-bye. Even so, she had faltered with those few words she'd murmured. In the early autumn breeze, her leaves fluttered like paper butterflies. Soon they would turn lemon yellow and fall softly to the earth. Perhaps she thought she would not see him again, that he would not return in her lifetime. All he had ever known was Stony Point, and he was filled with gloom at going away.

It didn't lessen his sadness all that much when goodScout retrieved him from the floor of the car and placed him beside her on the seat. The child would exclaim again how beautiful the stone was and the woman would look over and agree in a preoccupied sort of way. The child noticed everything, it seemed.

"Aunt Olive, look at those three geese up there. It almost looks like they are following us."

The geese did fly along for a time. Swift and mighty creatures that they were, they could not follow for long. He recognized the voices of Silverdew and his two friends.

They sounded so forlorn, calling, "good-bye, good-bye, come back soon, Skeedad." After a while, their voices trailed off, and all that could be heard was the heavy drone of the car.

Onward they drove, past the small town, past the farm fields of harvested corn, and cows plodding through pastures, past solitary human dwellings and tiny lakes surrounded by pine woods. Puffs of jolly clouds winked at them along the way.

And so began the long journey south for Skeedad. There was not a touch of water or a hint of anything green and growing. They traveled on and on as the day aged from dawn to dusk. The woman and child spoke of so many things that their conversations began to sound like the babbling brook of the inner creek. Skeedad tried to keep up with it. He thought if he could just listen long enough he would come to understand why they took him away, but he began to feel a slumbering numbness overtake him like winter, and he dozed.

By nightfall, the woman took him from goodScout, who had never let the stone out of her sight. GoodScout watched her intently as the woman casually dropped Skeedad into a small suitcase, where he spent the remainder of the journey in smooth darkness with dozens of unfamiliar objects.

"Hello? Is anyone there?" he whispered to the soft textured things around him. He was nestled in so snuggly he could barely see around the interior.

"Anyone at all?" he tried again, louder. "I am Skeedad of Stony Point, and I'm not supposed to be here. I belong beside the Blue Water."

Thunk! All of a sudden, the suitcase was moved, and he was rolled to the side with several other objects. The soft textured things stayed where they were, but suddenly he was face to face with a square ticking creature. It was the same size as he was, but it was cold and mechanical. Even its shape was peculiar to Skeedad.

"Tick, tock, tick tock, tick tock," it replied.

"Hello. I was just saying, I belong at the lakeshore. Do you know where they are taking us?" Skeedad asked hopefully.

"Tick tock, tick tock, tick tock, tick tock," came the answer.

"Well, I don't mean to offend you, but that really doesn't help. I mean, where exactly is Tick Tock? Oh dear, I most definitely do not belong here," Skeedad sighed. He knew his words were lost on this tick tock thing, so he kept quiet and tried harder to listen to his surroundings.

He heard raindrops on the car once and maybe even a bird singing in the far distance, but the sounds were muffled. The woman and child continued talking and laughing. There was no sound from goodScout, although Skeedad was sure she was still there.

Despite the boxed-in darkness, he knew that there had been at least two sunrises and sunsets and that the air was different. It was heavy, like thick warm mud. The car grumbled onward. They had already traveled very far and did not seem close to stopping.

He had so much time to think that he relived many things in great detail. The further the car traveled, the further he traveled into his own road of memories.

He thought about Whisperleaf as a young tree, inquisitive and attentive. She was the wisest and the most gentle of all the cottonwoods that had ever lived on Stony Point. She was also the eldest.

Skeedad thought fondly of Meadowsteps, the white-tailed deer, when she'd first appeared as a wobbly fawn with her mother and brother. Her mother taught the eager young fawns how to step lightly along the shore. Meadowsteps was not even a yearling when she arrived without her mother or brother one dark autumn day. She was solemn and barely drank from the lake. Something unspeakable had happened to her family. From then on, the stones were her dearest friends. She lingered by the water's edge well into the day. The stones knew better than to ask her what might have happened, and thankfully, Silverdew, who would have, was not there at the time.

Silverdew could not quite learn to think before speaking his mind. It was just his way. After all, his life had not been easy. He'd lost his mate long before, and he lived solely as a sentry goose. His life was dedicated to warning his two companion geese of any approaching trouble. He had to be alert at all times. There was not usually time to be courteous. More than once his boisterous voice had saved them from danger. They were truly grateful and quietly tolerated his bluntness. Skeedad missed the three geese.

And Solosong. Skeedad believed that the crow was more devoted to Stony Point than any crow before him. True, he was powerless to save them from danger, but he could warn them of it, and he always did. He appeared aloof and at times seemed quite arrogant. But the stones knew better. It was just Solosong's way. This, too, Skeedad missed.

Yes, he could imagine all of them. Blue Heron wading in the shallow water, pretending to ignore the ancient tales told most likely by other stones. Maybe it would be Skylo, the small red stone, who would be the one to weave a lively story based on days gone by. And everyone would listen attentively.

Everyone loved the story of Stony Point because it had no beginning and no end. Their world was simple and true, and there was good in everything when one learned to look for it. Things changed, and yet somehow things remained the same. The sun always set in the evening on the western shore and rose up over the treetops from the east the following dawn. Winter would always blanket them in snow, then melt into deep greens again in the spring. For some, there would be many more sunrises than for others. All the lake creatures knew and accepted that. The stones had seen more sunrises and more moonlight than anyone. Now, as the big car rumbled along, for the first time ever, Skeedad wondered about the good and where he would find it.

Just as he was considering this, the car jolted to a stop and goodScout barked happily. There was a flurry of activity, and Skeedad felt the suitcase being carried into some sort of human dwelling. He could hear voices and movements that made no sense to him. Time passed slowly. The tick tock thing next to him had finally stopped ticking. Was

it listening, too? Skeedad waited in the darkness,
wondering.

All at once, there was a rush of light as the
suitcase opened wide. He saw goodScout and the
child peering in to look. Then another child
appeared beside them.

"Look at this beautiful stone Scout found!"

"This? What's so beautiful about some old
rock?"

Rock? Skeedad had heard that word once
before. It was a human word. He thought it meant
a type of stone made by humans, although the
very idea was strange to him. He knew that he was
not a rock.

The child glanced appreciatively at Skeedad
and said, "Well, it was beautiful. It came from the
lake. There are millions of them. Scout liked this
one the best."

"Beautiful? It's just some old rock. Put it away.
Let's go," the other child said, turning away.

"I think it's a pretty stone. I don't care what
you think!" the first child exclaimed reaching into
the suitcase and picking up Skeedad. GoodScout
sniffed the stone and began to whine.

"It's okay, Scout. I'll put your stone in the desk
drawer where it will be safe," she said as Skeedad
felt himself being placed into a wooden drawer.
Before the drawer was shut, he looked up to see a
large gray bird glaring down at him with piercing
light-colored eyes. The bird had a curved black
beak and bright red tail feathers. It was not nearly
as large as Blue Heron, but it had that same look of
stern reproach. It had the air of Solosong's
haughtiness but seemed more hawk-like than
anything. Oddly, it was caged in some sort of wire
enclosure.

"Put it away, put it away. Old rock, old rock!" Skeedad was shocked to hear the bird speak human words.

"Don't be mean, Mr. Littlejohn." The first child spoke directly to the colorful bird.

How peculiar, Skeedad thought. Humans did not ordinarily speak with creatures. In fact, they never seemed to hear creatures speak. Never once did a human gaze into the face of a stone. They just couldn't see or hear the same things. Of course, the stones knew to close their eyes and retreat into themselves when humans were near, but that was just an extra precaution learned many ages ago. This conversing bird was another matter. It was something too unusual for him to understand yet.

As the drawer closed him into darkness, he heard the bird say mockingly, "Mean Mr. Littlejohn, mean Mr. Littlejohn," then, "old rock, put it away, put it away!"

Inside the drawer it was blacker than a moonless night and Skeedad felt he was lost forever. How would he ever get home to Stony Point? Would he ever see his friends again? Was goodScout trustworthy? He believed she did have a gentle and kind spirit. This was her home. He heard her trotting from the room with the children. It was quiet then.

It was so quiet that it unsettled him. For a very long time he listened to the emptiness. He wondered again why they had taken him away, claiming that he was so beautiful, only to put him here in this dark musty place. The stones never thought of themselves as beautiful. They were stones, wise and solid. They had knowledge that grew with the ages. That was their beauty.

What good could he find here? He listened so long and so intently to the silence that he entered a state of near slumber and began to hear the lake waves in his mind. Then, the voices of Whisperleaf and Solosong and even Silverdew filled the emptiness. It was autumn there now. How would he ever know the change of seasons, the approach of storms, the rising and setting of the sun? What could he learn from this? There wasn't anything but silent darkness. It was just a wooden drawer that smelled of old bark. He closed his eyes and began to retreat into his deepest memories to comfort himself. He would need to discover a path home.

"Hullo? Skeedad of Stony Point?" whispered a light melodic voice, interrupting the stillness.

Startled, Skeedad peered into the darkness and saw the outline of a huge feather. It was a giant goose feather. Next to the feather he could make out the shape of a seashell.

"Halloo. Skeedad of Stony Point. I am Deweye and this is Daysee of Stony Point," the feather announced, moving closer to the stone, who did not speak at first because he thought he was dreaming.

"Hello, Deweye and Daysee, I am glad to see you," he said hesitantly.

The feather, Deweye, had fluffed himself to an impressive size, causing the seashell to appear even more fragile and delicate. What an unusual pair, thought Skeedad, still trying to adjust to these surprise companions.

"Yes, yes, yes, you think you are dreaming, but you are not. We are short timers of Stony Point. We know you because you are a stone, the bravest and wisest of all," Deweye continued, bending dramatically to one side as if to bow.

"Well, the wisest and bravest, I don't know..." Skeedad said. Daysee interrupted him. Her words were like carefully measured bits of sand.

"Skeedad, sir...we welcome you."

Deweye chuckled. He lowered his voice to a meaningful whisper and hissed, "Yes, we welcome you...to the Drawer of Forgotten Things!"

- 6 -

DRAWER OF FORGOTTEN THINGS

 A tiny streak of light broke through the entrance to the Drawer of Forgotten Things. It was just enough light to illuminate Skeedad's new companions and their surroundings. He was becoming accustomed to the dimness of this strange world. Deweye dramatized all his words, while Daysee spoke with polite softness. Skeedad knew the two were short-timers of Stony Point; they would have followed a fleeting path for only a few seasons. There was good in that. But here, in this dark dry place, they would be long-timers. They were not meant to be long-timers. It was not natural. How could any of this be good?

As he was pondering this, Deweye and Daysee studied him intently. After a moment, Daysee spoke.

"We want to go home. We want to find the way north." She sounded so forlorn. It was as though she had given up hope of returning home and now just recited the words.

"I want to warm myself in the summer sun by the water's edge," she added dreamily.

Skeedad sensed her hopelessness. How long had they been here?

They could only tell him that it had been a very long time, that they had been brought here by humans for their natural beauty, but then had been left and forgotten. They wanted to hear stories of Stony Point, but Skeedad wanted to learn more about the Drawer of Forgotten Things. Most of all, he wanted to figure out how they might escape. He had to think. There had to be a way. There was always a way, but he had to know more.

Deweye became impatient with the momentary silence. He fluffed and preened. When he could wait no more, he began to talk about himself.

"It's true, of course, I am only a feather, yes, a short-timer. You would think that I would not have feelings on this subject of returning home, but I do!"

All of a sudden he began to sing.

> *"I am Dew-Eye*
> *Light and swift*
> *I spin, then fly,*
> *And dream to drift*
> *In the summer sky,*
> *The breeze will lift*
> *Me up so high*
> *What an honor*
> *To be Dew-Eye..."*

Daysee joined in and together they sang louder and louder, *"What an honor to be Dew-Eye, what an honor to be Dew-Eye..."*

Deweye paused, while Daysee continued humming the little tune. He eyed his companions and spoke in a booming voice.

"Listen, all I ever wanted was to be just what I am. A feather. Yes, that's right. Just a feather. A goose feather meant to be swept away in the first strong breezes of summer, to twirl and turn and fly high above Whisperleaf, to touch the sky, and travel on and on, forevermore."

While Skeedad was considering Deweye's words, the feather suddenly whirled around and asked him, "May I show you around the Drawer of Forgotten Things, Skeedad of the Blue Water Stones?"

"Yes, please. I must see," Skeedad said.

"Well then, this way sir," the feather said with a sweep and a bow. He moved slowly, allowing the stone time to roll along. Daysee stayed by Deweye's side.

"First, there is the Box of Forgotten Places. Go ahead, look inside. It will surprise you."

The Box of Forgotten Places was not much taller than Skeedad. It was plain and made of something foreign to him. The top was open slightly, and he peered inside. He was astonished to see rainbows and sunshine, deep blue skies with huge white clouds and sunsets on the lake. There were red, yellow, and orange leafed trees and a blue heron frozen in flight above the cattails. Behind each miniature forgotten place was another and another.

Each of the forgotten places was completely still. Not one thing moved. How could that be possible? He saw the small town, the farm fields and plodding cows. He saw the tiny lakes and the pine woods. He was awestruck. The forgotten places seemed to go on forever. Skeedad wanted to look away. It was too much to understand.

"Next is the Box of Forgotten Humans," Deweye said, moving ahead while Skeedad continued staring into the first box.

"Ahem! The Box of Forgotten Humans is next," Deweye repeated. He flitted back to where Skeedad was. Skeedad followed along reluctantly, still looking back at the first box.

The Box of Forgotten Humans was the same size as the Box of Forgotten Places, and again Skeedad found it slightly open. He peered inside. He was shocked to see the smiling face of Brookdweller staring at him. Skeedad quickly backed away.

"How is it possible that—" he started, searching Deweye for an answer.

"Go ahead. Take your time. You will find it fascinating," Deweye said. He watched Skeedad move closer to the box, then slowly peek inside again.

Yes, it was Brookdweller. He was a young man, and he was surrounded by other humans. All seemed happy and were laughing. They were so tiny. One of the tiny humans was holding up a miniature fish from the water on some sort of string thing. It was startling to see it. And the most eerie thing was that no one actually moved. They, too, were frozen in place. Behind them were even more humans, all smiling and all gaping at him. And there was another Brookdweller, except older, and not smiling. And then, still another Brookdweller sitting, a Brookdweller walking, and a Brookdweller standing. He was shorter than Skeedad. How could that be?

Just as he thought he had seen enough, Daysee tapped at the next box, which she explained was the Box of Forgotten Sounds. There was a slight hiss, then a melody unlike any he had heard from Blue Water songbirds or loons or even the distant coyotes. He listened, mesmerized. It was a peaceful sound, but it stopped almost as suddenly as it had begun.

"Again?" Daysee asked as she tapped against the Box of Forgotten Sounds, which started the tune once again. This time it played a bit longer, and they fell silent in reverence to its song.

"There's more..." Deweye interrupted.

"I want to see everything," Skeedad said, rolling along behind the feather who made dramatic sweeps this way and that.

"This," Deweye said, absently dusting a rectangular object, "is the Box of Forgotten Thoughts."

Skeedad stared at the box and could see that it had a front and a back bound together with a thick middle, which Deweye explained contained pages of human words that no one cared about anymore. This made no sense to Skeedad at all. He listened to Deweye tell him that the words were a human's thoughts written onto pages and pages and then forgotten. This made even less sense to Skeedad.

"Now, over here is the Box of Forgotten Time." Deweye was showing him a tick tock creature, just like the one Skeedad had traveled with, only it wasn't making a sound. It just sat there, dusty and unmoving.

Deweye said it was called a clock and that the Box of Forgotten Thoughts was called a journal. The Box of Forgotten Places and the Box of Forgotten Humans contained something called photographs. He was not able to explain the Box of Forgotten Sounds. Deweye was about to show Skeedad more when Skeedad stopped him.

"Deweye and Daysee, may I ask, how do you know all this?" Skeedad asked amazed.

"Oh. Um, well, we learned it all from OldSkogmo," Deweye replied casually.

Skeedad gasped. How could they have learned from OldSkogmo? OldSkogmo was taken away by humans long ago when Whisperleaf was still a young tree. No one had seen or heard about him since.

As though reading his thoughts, Daysee whispered, "OldSkogmo is here...in the Drawer of Forgotten Things, Skeedad, sir."

"What? Where? And how?" Skeedad asked. This was unbelievable!

"There," she whispered, looking to the back of the drawer.

Skeedad followed her gaze. What he saw was both alarming and a source of joy. It was indeed OldSkogmo. He was all the way at the back of the drawer in the darkest corner. Yes, it was OldSkogmo, alright. There was no mistaking the orange and black speckles and the smooth round shape. Skeedad was filled with hopefulness. And yet, he saw that OldSkogmo was dull and lifeless. His eyes had been closed a very long time, and he did not respond in any way as the three moved closer to him.

"OldSkogmo? It's me, Skeedad," he called to his friend.

"Oh, poo, he can't hear you. He's become a rock!" Deweye announced.

"Deweye! Don't say that!" Daysee hissed. "OldSkogmo is just resting!"

"Yes, forevermore," Deweye chortled, lowering his voice.

"A rock? A rock! He cannot be a rock because he is a stone. A Blue Water stone," Skeedad exclaimed. "And that is forevermore!"

"Well, I don't know, Skeedad, sir. He used to talk with us and tell us incredible tales, all true, and all first-hand accounts. He wasn't always in the Drawer of Forgotten Things. I don't know when he came to be here exactly," Deweye said.

He looked towards OldSkogmo and added, "Before he was left in this drawer, he discovered a lot about humans from being in their world. He once said that it was such a tiresome thing to be a paperweight, but he learned all he could from listening to Brookdweller. Somehow, he was able to find good in everything around him. He was put here after Brookdweller went to be above the sky."

Brookdweller above the sky? Was that possible, Skeedad wondered. He could hardly imagine humans above the sky. They were always so unable to rest long enough to truly absorb goodness. It just didn't seem likely. But then, Brookdweller was exceptional.

"When we came to be here, OldSkogmo was very kind and helped us to find good. It wasn't easy," Daysee said. "I believe that as so very many sunrises came and went, he drifted into a state of winter's deepest slumber and has not returned. But," she added, with a stern look in Deweye's direction, "he did not become a rock!"

Ashamed, Deweye spoke more softly to Skeedad. "Do you think you can bring him back? He's been silent for a long, long time. Ages."

Skeedad studied OldSkogmo. It was still OldSkogmo; he was still in there. "I will stay with him and remind him of the lakeshore. I'll try."

It was a somber sight. Skeedad stayed beside OldSkogmo well into the sunrise without a word spoken. Deweye and Daysee reluctantly left the two stones at the back of the Drawer of Forgotten Things and waited. They knew that any hope for OldSkogmo's return would come from what Skeedad might do.

Several more sunrises and sunsets passed, and still Skeedad stayed with his silent friend. Stones are very patient creatures, Daysee reminded Deweye.

One day though, he did leave OldSkogmo. He had to. There was a distracting commotion at the entrance to the Drawer of Forgotten Things. When he got there, he discovered Deweye and Daysee singing along to the melody of the Box of Forgotten Sounds. They were belting out the song as loud as they could.

"I am Dew-Eye
Light and swift,
I spin, then fly
And dream to drift—"

Suddenly there was a loud tapping outside the drawer, which became more persistent. The pounding was so loud that the two stopped singing at once.

"Uh oh," Deweye gulped.

The drawer creaked open slightly, allowing a shaft of blinding light to enter, as a voice snapped, "Be quiet! That is a stupid song, and I am sick of it! You will not be allowed to sing it again. Do you understand? I have spoken!"

It took Skeedad a moment to realize who was speaking to them. It was the large gray talking bird he had seen when he'd first entered the Drawer of Forgotten Things. Deweye and Daysee were cringing with fear and said nothing.

"It's not a stupid song. It's a good song. Why do you not want them to sing it?" Skeedad asked politely.

"Are you speaking to me, old rock?" the bird shrieked.

"Yes. Why, yes I am. You are Mr. Littlejohn? I am Skeedad of the Blue Water Stones. I am a stone. I am not a rock," Skeedad replied.

"How dare you speak out of turn! I am Lord Littlejohn to you, you boring old rock. Rocks are boring. You are boring me! Now, I want quiet in this Drawer of Forgotten Things this instant!" And with that he began to hammer on the drawer with his powerful beak until it closed.

Skeedad was aghast. As the light in the drawer was reduced to the dimness he'd become accustomed to, he turned to his companions.

"Deweye, Daysee, you must not be afraid. Mr. Littlejohn is a very troubled bird," Skeedad said. "Something is not right about him. Go ahead, sing your song, and I will go sit with OldSkogmo for a bit."

Deweye and Daysee didn't budge. They stared after Skeedad in awe of his bravery. He'd stood up to the mean Mr. Littlejohn. Just as they began to feel safe from the bird, the drawer flew open wide. There was the child, Lottie, peering in at them.

"There you are pretty stone," she said, picking up Skeedad. She admired the stone, holding him to the light, and then to everyone's amazement she tucked him into her jacket pocket.

Uh oh, this cannot be good, Skeedad thought.

Off they went. It was soft and dark in the pocket. He was bounced around as the child skipped and ran. For a split second, he sensed that goodScout was at the child's side but then she said, "No, you have to stay here." And the dog stayed.

After a while she was joined by other children and still more children until all Skeedad could hear was a multitude of children talking and giggling. Then an adult voice sounded above them, and the children became quiet. The adult voice droned on and on until the children began whispering. Skeedad had no idea what to think. He waited.

After a short time, a loud bell rang and the children began shrieking and laughing. The child lifted him out of her pocket and held him in her outstretched hand for all the children to see.

"See? It's a beautiful stone from way up north," she said.

"Can I have it, Lottie?" one child asked as he grabbed Skeedad from her.

"No, give it back," Lottie said.

Another larger child pushed forward and took the stone from the first child and said, "What's so special about it?"

"It's just an old rock," another child said.

The children all looked at Lottie. She snatched Skeedad back and hesitated, looking down at the stone. Skeedad could tell that Lottie was growing uncomfortable when all of a sudden she blurted, "Well, it's a magic stone!"

Magic? Skeedad wondered what that could possibly mean.

"Oh yeah? What does it do then?" sneered the large child.

Again, the children pressed forward and wanted to touch the magic stone. They gazed from the stone to Lottie, then back to the stone. They looked back at her again, expectantly.

"Well..." she paused, thinking, then said triumphantly, "it shows you the way north!"

"Big deal! I'll show it north," one child snatching the stone and tossing it high above him. Skeedad soared upwards, feeling oddly buoyant and weightless. He sailed higher and higher toward blue sky. He was a bird. He was Solosong or Silverdew ascending to the clouds above treetops. It was wonderful. Except that just when he thought he might make it to the moon, he began to fall. Down, down, faster and faster. He became dizzy, bracing himself for his crash to earth.

"How exactly does it show you the way north?" challenged the larger child, catching Skeedad just before he landed.

Lottie shifted and grew increasingly nervous. She thrust her chin forward and said, "It just does! You just have to know what to look for. It can show you the way north even if you are in total darkness or even if you are in a box, or well, anything like that."

She had no idea what she meant and neither did Skeedad. Although he did know the way north.

"It's not that great. It's just an orange and black stone," a small boy said. "It's not even a good skipper rock." He took the stone from the large child and held it up for everyone to agree.

In one quick movement, Lottie grabbed Skeedad, dropped him into her jacket pocket and bolted away from the other children.

"I don't care what you think. It was my dog who found the stone anyway!"

Skeedad wondered why Lottie became so glum after the others had scoffed at her. He was amazed by her sensitivity. Lottie had claimed he was beautiful because she saw him as a Stony Point stone. She still pictured him surrounded by other lake creatures under the shade of Whisperleaf as the blue water swirled around him like liquid laughter. To her, each stone had sparkled in its own unique way.

Skeedad knew the peace of Stony Point was soothing and constant and that the stones had absorbed it all. Lottie had tried to share a glimpse of this with the other children, but they could just not feel it. Skeedad recognized that, even if he had looked directly at the children and boldly announced himself, the children would not have been able to see him for who he was because they did not have the eyes or heart for it. Lottie couldn't change that.

Later that afternoon when Lottie returned home, GoodScout greeted her as she approached, but she barely spoke to the dog. When she finally arrived back at the old desk, she opened the Drawer of Forgotten Things and looked up at Mr. Littlejohn.

"It is an ugly old rock. Just an ugly old rock," she said.

Skeedad was dropped into the drawer with a thud. Lottie closed the drawer and he was left in the dark. As she walked away, he heard Mr. Littlejohn whisper to him, "Ha! Now, you really belong in the Drawer of Forgotten Things!"

- 7 -

MR. LITTLEJOHN

━━━━━━━━━━━━━━━━━━━━◯▬◯━━━━━━━━━━━━━━━━━━━━

As autumn gave way to winter, the north wind howled furiously. Deweye said that the wind, which could be heard despite being inside the Drawer of Forgotten Things, called his name. He knew it. He could hear "Deweye" clearly. He even answered. But his reply was lost as the glass window panes clattered from the icy air whistling through tiny cracks. The north was far away and dreamlike. Skeedad and Daysee would listen as Deweye would sing a song to the north wind.

The problem was that he would sing louder and louder until he was nearly shouting. Daysee could not stop herself from joining in, and it always happened that Mr. Littlejohn's voice would boom above them as he worked the drawer open with his beak.

"Stop it, Stop it, Stop it! How many times do I have to tell you?" he shouted impatiently. He peered in at them with his sharp eyes.

It was always the same. Skeedad would try to talk with the bird, but Mr. Littlejohn would become even more irritable, telling them that he was the ruler of the Drawer of Forgotten Things, and they had better do as he said, or else.

"Or else what?" Skeedad asked one day, wondering what could be worse than being in the dark drawer forever.

"I do not have to answer that," the large bird replied angrily and using his beak, pushed the drawer shut one jab at a time.

They never saw Lottie. She had not returned since the time she called Skeedad an ugly old rock. GoodScout's pattering footsteps were heard sometimes in the distance. OldSkogmo remained in a state of slumber while Skeedad stayed by him, certain that someday he could reach his friend.

"Skeedad, sir…I believe that OldSkogmo could no longer find good in anything. That's why he is, well…gone," Deweye explained one day. He said this in his kindest voice. Daysee felt differently and said so.

"Gone? No, he still has good inside. He's just resting. It's what stones do, right?" She turned to Skeedad.

"You are both right," Skeedad answered sadly. "OldSkogmo has been missed at Stony Point for a long, long time. He'll never be forgotten. He was so very sensible. He used to tell us all sorts of things from old legends that only he could remember. There was this lively way he had of storytelling what could hurl you back in time. I think it was because he could see and hear more than anyone else, and he remembered everything. I mean everything. He didn't miss even one falling leaf! Brilliant, he was just brilliant," he added.

For a while they did not speak. Finally Daysee said, "He still is a brilliant stone. Anyone can see that. He told us that the child who took him from the lakeshore used to speak to him as though she could actually see him. Can you imagine? As if she could see him! When she grew up, she gave him to her grandfather, Brookdweller, to keep on this desk as a paperweight."

"A paper what? What is *that*?" Skeedad asked.

"No, no, a *paper weight*!" Daysee said.

"Paper wait? What were the papers waiting for?" Skeedad was puzzled.

"No, no, not that kind of waiting. Well, sort of that, but also to keep the papers from getting away, I guess," Daysee replied, now a little puzzled herself.

"Paper wait? Now, that's just strange. Why would papers try to leave? What did he have to do to get them to stay? Just sit there?" Skeedad asked, curious to know the fate of his friend.

"No. Well yes, to hold down the Forgotten Papers whenever the north wind blew through the open window, I presume. The Forgotten Papers are here in the Drawer of Forgotten Things. I could show them to you. Maybe they might tell us the way north. OldSkogmo knew what the papers were. I know he told us. I just don't remember. Daysee, do you remember?" Deweye said.

"Papers and papers and papers of forgotten things. I'm not sure, Deweye. OldSkogmo said the papers were very important to Brookdweller," Daysee said.

"Forgotten papers..." Skeedad repeated thoughtfully. He just could not understand why there were so many forgotten things. Forgotten places, forgotten humans, forgotten time, forgotten sounds, forgotten thoughts, forgotten papers.

At Stony Point every single thing, tiny or huge, short-timers or long-timers, rainstorms or sunshine, had significance and value. It was all important. It all mattered. The stones knew this better than anyone because they had been there so long that they understood how, over time, things worked together to become good. It was really quite simple.

Deweye and Daysee were looking at him.

"So, what about Mr. Littlejohn? What do you know about him," Skeedad asked, changing the subject, "Don't you think it's a bit peculiar that a large bird lives in such a place?"

"He's not like any other bird we've ever known," Daysee replied.

"He doesn't fly away," Deweye added. "What good are his wings if he never uses them to fly away? He's quite mean and..."

"Lonely?" Skeedad added.

"Yes! Lonely! He must be very lonely," Daysee exclaimed.

"No one comes to see him?" Skeedad asked.

"Nope! He's too mean. Doesn't have one nice thing to say. Ever," Deweye said.

"No one? Ever?" Skeedad was stunned.

"Maybe no one visits him because he always says such horrible things. The little girl used to talk to him. Sometimes he just ignored her and sometimes he would say hateful things. She really did try though," Daysee said.

"Maybe he misses Brookdweller. OldSkogmo told us that he really only liked Brookdweller," Deweye said.

"Brookdweller? Hmmm...Mr. Littlejohn must be very old then. Almost a human lifetime." Skeedad pondered this.

"OldSkogmo also told us that Mr. Littlejohn wasn't always so mean. You know, you're right. He must be lonely! Don't you agree, Deweye," Daysee asked, turning to her friend.

"Well, I suppose..." Deweye said reluctantly, then added, "What does it matter? He's mean now!"

Daysee and Deweye looked glum. Mr. Littlejohn had tormented them for as long as they could remember. The worst part was that they never really knew why. It didn't matter if they were quiet or loud, polite or rude. The bird was always mean to them.

Suddenly Skeedad's mood brightened. "I have an idea. Come with me. We are going to talk to him."

"Oh, no! Oh no, no, no, no, no, no...he could hurt us," Deweye exclaimed, backing away from Skeedad.

"Deweye! Do you want to find the way north?"

"No! Well, okay, I meant...yes, yes, I do," Deweye said cautiously.

"Then, don't you see? We have to try talking to Mr. Littlejohn. He may know something important. In any case, he likely has a lot of good inside that needs to come out," Skeedad said.

"I sincerely doubt that," Deweye muttered.

Ignoring Deweye, Skeedad said in a gentle voice, "I believe that Mr. Littlejohn has forgotten his own good."

The three made their way to the front of the drawer with Skeedad in the lead. Deweye was so hesitant that Daysee had to push him with all her might.

"Hullo? Mr. Littlejohn?" Skeedad said.

There was no reply. They could hear the big bird moving about, but he did not answer.

"Hello? We would like to speak with you, please, Mr. Littlejohn," Skeedad shouted. Still the bird refused to answer.

"Okay! This is what we must do." Skeedad turned to his friends and said, "We need to sing that song. You know, the one you sing the most. Look, I will sing it with you."

"Ahem...*I am Dew-Eye, light and swift...*" Skeedad began. At first he was the only one singing but Deweye and Daysee finally chimed in, unable to resist singing their favorite song. Skeedad's voice was strong and deep. The three sang louder and louder. Deweye twirled as he sang and Daysee harmonized in her high-pitched voice. Louder and louder they sang. It wasn't long before they were belting out the song at the top of their voices.

Bam! Bam! Bam! Mr. Littlejohn pried the drawer open with his powerful beak and feet. He backed off a little when he saw that the three were at the very front of the drawer.

"Stop it! Stop the stupid song! Stop it now!" He screeched so loud that Deweye was flipped backwards into the drawer.

Skeedad ignored this. Instead he asked, "Mr. Littlejohn, what kind of bird are you? We have never seen such a colorful bird who can talk directly to humans."

Mr. Littlejohn eyed Skeedad suspiciously. "Why do you want to know?"

"Just do," Skeedad replied.

"Just do, just do....just do," Mr. Littlejohn repeated. He was searching for something hateful to say, but instead he found himself saying, "Just do, eh? I am an African Grey parrot!"

"Where are you from?" Skeedad asked, relieved that the parrot had not said anything mean.

"South. South of the world. I am an African Grey parrot from the deepest forests of Africa. Very, very, very far south. South of the world." He glared at Skeedad as though the question was meant as a challenge.

Deweye was shocked that the parrot was answering questions so easily. He moved forward, bowed slightly and asked the parrot in a croaking voice, "Um, well, then, why don't you just fly away to south of the world?"

Mr. Littlejohn jerked his head in Deweye's direction and snapped, "Because I am here and I am the ruler of the Drawer of Forgotten Things. You will go back and leave me alone now, this instant!"

Deweye was horrified. He had not intended to anger the parrot, but he had. Before Skeedad had a chance to ask anything more, Mr. Littlejohn slammed the drawer shut.

It was a very long time before they spoke with the parrot again. He would scold them from outside the drawer but refused to open it when they asked.

The blackness of winter passed into spring, and they could hear birds twittering somewhere outside, far away. A time of great rain came and all they heard was water driving down from the sky. It was then that Skeedad decided to try again to befriend the lonely old parrot. He had a new plan.

Early one morning, Skeedad began calling for goodScout. He called and called. His voice was low and determined. He believed that eventually the dog would hear him and would come to investigate.

"GoodScout! Over here, it's this way," he called softly.

After what seemed like a very long time, goodScout trotted into the room and sat by the desk with her head cocked to one side listening to her name being called.

Mr. Littlejohn screamed at her to go away. He told her she was a bad, horrible dog and that she had no business sitting by the old desk. GoodScout whined, not understanding. But, there it was again. Someone was calling her.

"GoodScout! Come here...can you help us?"

How unusual, thought the dog. She glanced up at Mr. Littlejohn who glared down at her.

"GoodScout, it's us. You remember, from the Blue Water."

GoodScout did remember the lake. She remembered the stone from the lakeshore. Yes, yes. That was it. It was the stone's little voice calling her from within the desk drawer. Then she remembered the time when she and Lottie were lost in the storm and those same little voices helped her find the way back. It had been the stones who spoke to her that day.

All of a sudden the old parrot decided to work the drawer open with his beak. He was furious!

"Why, why, why must you persist in annoying me? Don't you get it? You are in this Drawer of Forgotten Things because you are forgotten. That means you are nothing, and you need to behave like nothing. It means you must say nothing, you must do nothing, and you must sing nothing. You are nothing! Nothing, nothing, nothing but forgotten things," Mr. Littlejohn shouted.

GoodScout looked on in amazement. She did not budge.

"Please, we just want to ask you some questions. Please don't shut the drawer, Mr. Littlejohn," Skeedad pleaded.

"Well, for pity's sake, what is it? What, what, what do you want to know? Be brief!" The parrot was exasperated.

"Um, for one thing, we want to know—" Deweye, who was hiding behind Skeedad, began.

Skeedad interrupted Deweye, "—we want to know if you will assist us in finding the way back north."

"What? Are you seeds and nuts? Why in Africa's name would I do such a thing," the parrot screeched while goodScout continued to watch in disbelief.

"Well, I mean, don't you ever want to go home? To the south? To the deep forests of Africa? Don't you have friends and family there?" Skeedad asked cautiously.

Unexpectedly, the parrot looked away for a moment. He gazed out the window at the steady warm rain of late spring and said nothing. When he did speak, his tone changed slightly.

"They have forgotten me by now," he replied quietly.

"Oh, surely not! A regal parrot such as yourself? How long have you been gone?" Daysee asked.

Mr. Littlejohn continued to stare out the window and muttered, "A lifetime."

"What's it like? The south," asked Deweye carefully, afraid he might say the wrong thing again and make Mr. Littlejohn angry.

"Ah, it's paradise. Warm and abundant. It rains the most fragrant rain you could imagine. And colorful. Bright and so much green." The parrot's mood had become pensive, almost forlorn.

"Yes, yes, but what about Lottie? She is the great granddaughter of Brookdweller, your friend. Why are you so mean to her? You're just always so—" Deweye said without thinking. He stopped himself and cringed slightly, waiting for a reproach.

But it was as though the old parrot could only hear and see memories of his youth at that moment because he did not answer Deweye. Instead, he spoke almost to himself, "Humans came to the forest one day. They had giant brooms and began beating the trees. When I tried to fly away, I was captured in a huge net and stolen away from my homeland. So young. I was so young. The other Greys got away. Then, I was smuggled north of the world for a huge sum of money. It was horrid. Just horrid. I lost my territory, my family, my paradise. I would have lived many, many ages there."

Slowly he turned and looked directly at Deweye. He seemed to finally hear his questions. Deweye hid behind Skeedad, waiting for the on-slaught of scolding.

"Brookdweller, you call him? Hmmm. Yes, he was a friend," Mr. Littlejohn said. "A human, yes, but a friend, nevertheless. He was old, as I am now. He rescued me from that ghastly pet store where it was said that I was too mean to touch. He didn't pay one penny for me. He walked in and said, 'you're a long way from home, fella,' which was true. He saw a speck of good in me from my life before and ignored the CAUTION sign on my cage. He let me be myself and treated me with great respect. He told the shop clerk that it was a tragedy that I was not left in my natural world. That pet store was glad to get rid of me. He brought me here. To his library. This was the place he spent his days. We became the best of friends. But then, he died, and I had nothing. Just nothing."

A dark gloom settled on him as he turned to look out the window again. Rain water trickled down the window pane in chaotic streaks. The sky was heavy and colorless.

"But what about Lottie?" Deweye asked. "She seems to want to be your friend. She's quite tender hearted and bright for a human."

"Oh, yes, her. I don't know," Mr. Littlejohn replied.

"And there's goodScout, the kindest of all dogs," Skeedad said.

The big yellow dog wagged her tail when she heard this. The parrot gazed at her as though seeing her for the first time. The dog had never caused him any harm.

"Mr. Littlejohn, if you sing a song and act as though you feel cheery, before you know it…well, you will be," Daysee exclaimed, adding, "That's what we do."

"Yes, yes, I know. The song. The stupid song," he groaned, growing restless. He didn't want to talk any more. He just wanted to watch the rain fall.

He ended the conversation without another word, shutting the drawer more slowly than usual.

When Deweye tried to protest, Skeedad hushed him to silence. He knew Mr. Littlejohn needed to retreat to himself and ponder many things.

GoodScout remained beside the old parrot, sensing his need for her quiet presence. She settled on a small rug for a nap. She would do this many times before summer. Mr. Littlejohn became accustomed to her company, taking comfort in the dog's goodness.

Many days and nights passed and still Mr. Littlejohn stared out the window. He thought of his youth, of his home. Never could he return. So much time had passed. Was it true what OldSkogmo had told him after Brookdweller died? He had said to look for the good, no matter what. If you stopped looking for good, you would die inside. The seashell, Daysee, told him to act cheery, to sing a song, and that he would begin to feel cheery. It seemed absurd. Ridiculous, really. He looked at goodScout napping on the floor below him. She was a human's pet, and yet...

He thought of Lottie. The little girl had spent countless hours talking to him, bringing him special treats and toys. She had the same eyes as Brook-dweller. Eyes that could look into a creature's tortured soul and heal the hurt. She had not been the one to bring him here. She would not take him back south. He belonged here now. It had been his home for a long, long time. He had just stopped seeing any good in it.

He stretched his wings and lifted his head high. The rain had stopped and there was a yellow sun illuminating the fresh green leaves of early summer.

"La, La, La, La, La, La, La, La, La, La La-Lottie, Lala Lottie!" He sang so loud, he startled himself. GoodScout jolted awake and stood at attention.

"Oh lalalalalalalaLottie," he sang out again and again. Soon there was a muffled chorus coming from the Drawer of Forgotten Things and even goodScout yipped along.

"Lalalalalalalala Lottie, lalalalalala Lottie, lalalalalala Lottie, la la la la Lottie!" It wasn't much of a song, but it was a start. Sure enough, Lottie appeared in the room, her eyes wide and her mouth open in astonishment.

"Mr. Littlejohn?" she exclaimed. "Are you calling me?"

"Yes! Yes, I am! La, la, la, la Lottie! Gooooood morning!" he replied. He was elated that she had appeared so quickly.

"Gosh, well okay. Good morning to you, too, Mr. Littlejohn," she said, still surprised. She bounced over to him and stroked the top of his head, something she had not done in years.

It was as though he had never said one hateful thing to her. She stretched out her arm for him to climb onto, which he did gladly. He was very proud and continued to sing, "La, la, la, Lottie, my friend Lottie. My friend, Scout." This felt great! The dog trotted along as they pranced through the room. Mr. Littlejohn could not remember when he had felt so jubilant.

During the day, Lottie dashed in and out of the room bringing him treats and new silly toys, but mostly her company. She talked to him earnestly, the way one would talk to a good friend who had been away for years. It was unbelievable to him. At the days's end, she covered his cage with a blanket the way she had long ago. The cage door was left open, as usual, but she had covered the cage. It was a wonderful thing.

After dark, he thought once again of his home, far, far, south of the world. No, he would never go back. And although he would always miss it and always have that sadness, he would be fine here with Lottie and goodScout.

"Thank you, OldSkogmo, Thank you, Skeedad, Deweye, and Daysee," he whispered, "Thank you for teaching me to look for the good."

"You're welcome," came the immediate hushed reply from the closed drawer.

"I will never return south, but for the sake of all that is good and right, you will find your way north. And I will help you," he exclaimed in a voice strong with resolve. He, too, had a plan.

"Yippee! We are going home! Did you hear that? Home," shouted Deweye. "But how? How? How? I just want to know how. You must tell us. Because the way north is far, far away—"

"Shhhh—hush! You must not let the humans hear you. They will come in here thinking it is me chatting in the night. I do have a plan. It will work," replied the parrot. "But everyone must be very careful and do exactly as I say."

In his most quiet voice, Mr. Littlejohn called goodScout into the room. After a moment, she came in and sat by the desk, looking at him expectantly.

"Scout, there is something you must do," Mr. Littlejohn said. He spoke easily and expertly as though he had thought this plan over for a long time.

"Go to Lottie's room. Find the small travel case. The one she always packs for trips. Bring it to me. But, don't let anyone see you. Be very, very quiet. You must not awaken the child. Understand?" He spoke simply and clearly so there would be no mistake what he wanted goodScout to do.

GoodScout wagged her tail, spun around and pattered softly out of the room. The instant she was gone, Mr. Littlejohn began prying the Drawer of Forgotten Things open. He worked hard at opening the drawer as wide as he could. He looked at Deweye and Daysee. They were at the front eagerly anticipating the way out.

"Where is Skeedad?" the parrot asked. He saw that the stone had stayed to the back.

"We cannot leave OldSkogmo," Skeedad said firmly. "He must return to north, too. It's his only chance. I will not leave him."

"Yes, I know. I thought of that, too. If I could just get this drawer to open wider…" Mr. Littlejohn struggled with the drawer. It had been one thing to pry it open enough to scold them, but opening it wide enough to get to OldSkogmo was almost impossible. Halfway open, the drawer stuck. He could not get it to budge another inch.

"Can you push him to the front?" Mr. Littlejohn wondered aloud. OldSkogmo was at the darkest back corner.

"We can try," Skeedad said. They could. They could try, he thought, knowing that OldSkogmo was considerably bigger than any of them. Skeedad, Deweye, and Daysee exchanged looks. Without saying a thing, they began to make their way to the back of the drawer.

Mr. Littlejohn watched as they disappeared into the darkness of the Drawer of Forgotten

Things. He was doubtful but listened intently as they tugged and pushed and shoved and prodded. He heard grunts and groans and pleading.

They were getting nowhere, but there was no stopping them. Their determination was so powerful, Mr. Littlejohn started to believe they could do anything.

"It's no use," Deweye wailed from the back of the drawer. "We can't push him!"

"Now we will never find the way north," Daysee cried.

"Just hold on, you two. There must be something," Skeedad said.

He was interrupted by goodScout who entered the room dragging a travel case. She lifted it every few steps in an attempt to make less noise. Mr. Littlejohn was pleased to see that it was the right bag.

The dog froze when all of a sudden a light was turned on somewhere in the house. They heard footsteps coming toward the room. They all held their breath.

"Drop! Pretend to be asleep," Mr. Littlejohn hissed.

The footsteps came closer and closer. Suddenly a switch snapped on flooding the room with light.

"Anyone in here," Olive asked uncertainly. She clutched her robe to her and peered around the room, her gaze falling on goodScout. Rubbing her eyes, she reached down to pet the dog just as Mr. Littlejohn started to shriek.

Startled, Olive turned off the light and stepped back. After a moment, she switched on the light again and said, "What is wrong with you? You old coot. You scared me to death!"

"Bird sleeping! Bird sleeping! Bird sleeping!" Mr. Littlejohn screamed, trying to sound indignant.

"Oh goodness! Okay, Mr. Fussy Bird, I'm leaving." She glanced around the room again. For a moment she stared at the suitcase next to good-Scout, then shrugged. She patted the dog's head, turned off the light and left.

Skeedad, Deweye, Daysee, and goodScout waited for Mr. Littlejohn to speak.

"Excellent job, Scout!" he finally whispered. "Now, Scout, can you jump up and put your front feet here?" He pointed his beak to the drawer entrance, which was still halfway open.

GoodScout tipped her head to one side as though trying to understand why she would be asked to do such a thing. She wanted to help her friends. After all, hadn't they shown her the way out of the storm at the lakeshore?

Her hesitation caused Mr. Littlejohn to become anxious. Did she understand what he was asking? He tapped the drawer in repeated motion with his beak and even placed one foot inside the front of the drawer.

"Scout, please. Just slap your front paws right here. Nothing to it. You know, like when you were a puppy and humans told you not to jump on things," Mr. Littlejohn said.

Of course she understood. And, as the dog jumped up landing her big front paws on the drawer, it tipped slightly, hurling everyone to the front. Skeedad, Deweye, Daysee, and even OldSkogmo flipped and rolled altogether to the entrance.

"It's a miracle!" Deweye shouted. "Yippee! We are going—"

"Shhhhhhh! Deweye! Please...you must be very, very quiet. In fact, you cannot speak again until you arrive north," the old parrot cautioned. "Scout, listen. You see these four? Take each one, one by one, very, very carefully and place them in the travel case." Thankfully, the case was open and partially packed with vacation clothes.

GoodScout did as she was told. She began with OldSkogmo, the largest, then Skeedad. She was ever so gentle and placed each stone deep into the bag, hiding them under the clothing. She picked up Deweye with her little front teeth, barely touching him. For a split second she let go, and he drifted softly to the inside of the bag. With her nose she rooted around, lightly pushing him beneath the clothes.

"Okay, Scout, now you must be the most gentle you have ever been in your entire life. Daysee is strong of heart, but so fragile you could crush her," Mr. Littlejohn said.

The dog hesitated. She opened her mouth and scooped up the seashell with her tongue. It was easy. Hiding her in the travel bag was a bit tricky, but the dog did as she was told and lifted a small corner of clothing so the little seashell could hide securely in the softest compartment.

Done. It was done! Mr. Littlejohn hopped down from his perch onto goodScout's head and tapped her nose lightly with his beak. "You have done a very good thing, Scout. Now, you must take the bag back where you found it. Very, very quietly."

The dog gazed up at the old parrot sitting on her head and wagged her tail happily. She wanted to bark but knew not to. Everything had gone smoothly.

As the parrot climbed back up on the desktop, he stopped for a moment at the Drawer of Forgotten Things, shutting it one last time. Then looking back at goodScout he said, "See you again in the autumn, my friend."

For a moment he felt a little sad and whispered to the others, "Farewell brave lake creatures. Farewell OldSkogmo, may you awaken one day and know that there was good here after all. Farewell my dear friends, Skeedad, Deweye, and Daysee."

© C.J. Clark

- 8 -
THE WAY NORTH

 "Whisperleaf?"

"Yes, Skylo?" came the faint reply.

"Were you sleeping?"

"No, just resting a bit." The great cottonwood sighed, gazing down at the stones. The small red stone looked up at her inquisitively. All the stones seemed to be looking at her.

Her leaves were sparse and dry, her branches brittle. It had been a hard winter of deep snow and fierce blizzards, but she had survived. She had survived to greet the soft blue and lush green of summer, a shadow of her former self.

Whisperleaf watched as Meadowsteps, the white-tailed deer, drank deeply from the lake with her new fawn by her side. The deer looked up, blinking her giant brown eyes. She was teaching her fawn the ways of the lake creatures.

In the silence of the shallow water stood the ever solitary blue heron. He was motionless except for an occasional glance back at the shore to make certain that his presence was appreciated.

Whisperleaf looked to the east. Early dawn had slipped away. The new day's sun rose into the sky, sprinkling shimmering dots on the lake, which was very still. Every sound was magnified in the quiet of morning. The cottonwoods on either side of her had grown to an impressive size and could rustle their leaves without the slightest breeze. She felt content to hold on to the good earth with the younger cottonwoods while birds, insects, and little animals darted by. Each day unfolded differently from the one before. And yet all the days were the same. Whisperleaf rested.

"Whisperleaf?"

"Yes, Skylo?"

"What is it like to be so tall? To be able to see so far and feel the breezes so high?"

"Good. It is good. There is so much. The blue of the sky vanishes when I touch it. The clouds are just out of reach. The sun rises up over the woods in beams of broken light, bit by bit until it is full in the sky. Birds fly so close that I could tickle them. And the stones. There are stones as far as I can see. Big stones, little stones. Stones of a lakeshore, a lakeshore of stones."

Together they listened to the hushed morning. In the far distance they could hear geese calling. Whisperleaf swept her lowest leafed branch softly across the stones.

"Skylo?"

"Yes, Whisperleaf?"

"What is it like to be so ancient? To be, and to be, and to be, for so very long...to slumber under ice in winter and to be washed with warm water in summer, to see and to see and to see so very much for so very long."

"It is good, Whisperleaf. The sun always rises in the east and sets in the west. The moonlight shelters us at night. Every good thing is within us forevermore. The caw of the crows, the call of the geese, the loons and herons, the breath of every breeze that blows, the change of leaves in the spring and autumn... to be old with the elders, and new again with the young. All at the same time."

"Look over there, Whisperleaf," Skylo continued, looking to the lake as a flock of Canadian geese landed in the water. Slowly, the geese began to drift towards the shore. "It's Silverdew, with his two friends and their young goslings. Silverdew has many charges now. As their protector, the extra responsibility will change him some. He has truly become himself, no longer a daft young goose. It is the course of things. It is good."

The small flock of geese swam leisurely into shore, then waddled onto the sandy bank making cackling sounds. The little goslings awkwardly followed their parents to the shade under the cottonwoods. Silverdew stayed slightly behind, scanning the sky and horizon.

"Gaak back. Gaak, back home," he bellowed and stood tall, flapping his wings. He was pleased to bask in the peacefulness of Stony Point. He greeted everyone.

It was one of those days that lingered softly, like sleep. A northern summer day was like floating on a gentle wave, warming away the last chill of winter. There was balance. There was harmony.

But suddenly the peacefulness was shattered when Solosong landed lightly in Whisperleaf's uppermost bare branches. He did his best not to disturb her. He began calling a persistent and familiar warning.

"Cau—cau—caution! Humans coming from the south! Cau—cau—cau—caution! Soon, very soon, close, very close, caution! Cau—cau—cau— caution!"

Then he was gone. All the lake creatures were startled. The blue heron lifted his giant wings. Gliding close to the water, he made his way to the creek without looking back. Meadowsteps and her fawn sniffed the air for a moment, then kicked up their heels and bolted back into the forest. Silverdew and the other geese waddled back to the lake and began to swim slowly away. There was a shrill call of a loon from somewhere near the creek. Then all was still.

It wasn't long after Solosong's warning that the big noisy car rumbled over the grassy driveway, coming to a halt beside the old cabin. The humans had returned.

"Wait! Wait for me!" Lottie called to goodScout, who was bounding ahead to the lakeshore. The big yellow dog began nudging and sniffing the stones. She wagged her tail and darted up the bank back to the child, coaxing her to come along.

Lottie charged ahead then abruptly stopped. "Look at that! Oh no, look at the old cottonwood tree!"

Aunt Olive joined them by the lake and together they gazed up at Whisperleaf. Finally Aunt Olive said, "This old tree has been here all my life and probably longer. I just hate to see it die. Mr. Peterson will want to cut it down, you know."

Lottie placed her arm around Whisperleaf's trunk and said, "Why? Why can't it just be left alone? If we weren't here, it wouldn't have to be cut down because there would be no one to see it. It would just die where it lived and in its own way." To Lottie, the tree was still more alive than dead and still grand and still beautiful.

Aunt Olive looked from Lottie to goodScout to Whisperleaf and sighed, "You know what, Lottie? You're right. I won't let anyone talk us into cutting it down while it still has a bit of life in it. It's a fine and dignified old tree."

GoodScout was still rooting around in the stones as Lottie and Aunt Olive went to unpack. It was a chilly day with hardly any breeze, causing their voices to echo across the lake as they laughed and talked, carrying luggage from the car to the cabin.

And then it happened.

"This is strange. Aunt Olive, how do you suppose these things got into my suitcase?" Lottie stood over the small travel bag, which she had just unpacked.

"What is it?" Aunt Olive asked, coming into the room.

"Well, here's Scout's stone and a little seashell and this huge pretty feather and look, another stone, even larger."

"You must have left them there from last year's trip, don't you think?"

Lottie knew that couldn't be. In fact, she remembered taking the smaller stone to school and telling the other children that it was a magic stone. It shows you the way north, she'd told them. They hadn't believed her, and she'd put the stone back in her grandfather's desk drawer. She didn't know what to think.

"It's a magic stone. It shows you the way north..." Lottie mumbled softly.

"What? What did you say?"

Just then goodScout trotted with a sense of purpose into the room. Remembering Mr. Littlejohn's instructions, she took the stone from Lottie's hand and strode to the screen door. She pawed at the door, which opened easily. Then she made her way down the grassy bank to the lakeshore. Lowering her head, she placed Skeedad gently by the water's edge near Whisperleaf, next to the other stones. Then, relieved that she had completed her mission, she rolled on her back next to the stones, kicking her feet in the air.

Lottie and Aunt Olive followed goodScout. They watched her in amazement.

"Let's go get the other things and bring them down here, too," Lottie said. It shows you the way north, she kept thinking. She ran back to the cabin with Aunt Olive behind her.

Aunt Olive picked up the larger stone, turning it over and over in her hand and said, "This stone looks familiar somehow. How could that be? Isn't that odd?"

But Lottie was still thinking of the magic stone. It shows you the way north. She pondered the wonder of it. How? How did it do that? She would never know. She only knew that she had tossed the stone back in the drawer calling it an ugly old rock and now, somehow, it was here. It was here, up north, where it belonged.

Carefully she picked up the feather and seashell and walked back to the water's edge with Aunt Olive. Together they placed Daysee, Deweye, and OldSkogmo beside Skeedad just below Whisperleaf on the lakeshore.

GoodScout looked up at Olive and Lottie and yipped in approval. The echoing sound momentarily broke the silence of the morning. She sat beside them then, gazing out at the lake. The water was smooth glass. Tufts of snow white clouds hung motionless in the sky. Lottie and Olive stood so close to the lake's edge that they could see their reflections mirrored clearly in the still water. The immense quiet made time stand still. For a long moment, the woman and child contemplated their reflections in the lake.

Aunt Olive saw herself reflected as a child again, taking a stone from the lake, wanting to make the pretty stone her own possession. Lottie saw herself as an adult, placing the stone back where it belonged. Neither spoke.

"Aunt Olive," Lottie finally said, "do you see?"

Aunt Olive nodded, understanding.

They watched as a tiny ripple of blue water circled the stones. Instantly their vibrant colors were restored. The blue water stones shone like precious jewels. The seashell, too, glistened as bright as the north star. And the goose feather, even with no breeze, seemed to flutter lightly, its tones distinct and soft.

"The stones, the seashell, and even the feather are all beautiful once again," Lottie exclaimed. It really was magic! They had found the way north.

© C.J. Clark

- 9 -

BEYOND FOREVERMORE

Olive awoke to early daylight timidly peeking through the cabin's windows. The raucous calling of a blue heron echoed somewhere on the lake. Shivering slightly, she noticed the previous night's warm roaring fire had become cold ash. She stared at her empty cocoa mug resting on the arm of the rocking chair.

What time was it? Had she been sitting here all night? Her mind was muddled. She'd had the oddest dream. Or no, not a dream exactly. It must have been her grandfather's story, which now lay scattered in her lap. She must have drifted off to sleep. That was it. She'd been reading and fell sound asleep.

She rubbed her eyes. Why had she been so upset the evening before? All at once, a certain peace she had never known before enveloped her. She felt sheltered by it as though it were a protective cocoon.

Blue water stones in the drawer of forgotten things, she remembered suddenly. This image stayed with her as she stretched and yawned. The Drawer of Forgotten Things. Her grandfather had told her that he didn't want to become like a stone in her childhood drawer of forgotten things, that he would feel useless and out of his element. Yes, it would crush his spirit, she thought.

Olive stood up, carefully tucking the story pages under her arm, she walked to her bedroom. She opened the top drawer of her dresser and took a long deep breath. Inside the drawer were stones, seashells, a peacock feather, the top of a cattail reed, a piece of driftwood, and what appeared to be a Canadian goose feather. Everything looked dull and worthless. Why had she kept all this? She gently removed the entire drawer from the dresser, being careful not to disturb anything. Quietly closing the cabin door behind her, she carried her drawer of forgotten things to the water's edge .

By the time she reached the lake, her grandfather had awakened and silently watched her from the cabin window. He watched as she sat on the beach and one by one, delicately placed each stone, seashell, feather, driftwood piece, and cattail reed by the water's edge. After she had done this, she stood up and studied the horizon.

The wind had shifted to the south, causing the waves to change direction. They sloshed into shore one after another after another, washing over the objects Olive had placed there. She bent towards the water, extending her hand to the waves as though to stop them, if only for a moment. For a long time she stood motionless, watching the waves. She didn't know that her grandfather saw and understood that Olive had discovered how to see good in even the smallest things, and then, too, she was learning how to let go, and let things be as they are.

She sat on the ground below the old cottonwood tree, patted the pages of Lottie's story into place and began to read the last of it. As she began to read, Olive felt as though she could hear her grandfather's voice deep inside the waves as they tossed droplets of water at her, dancing to the liquid laughter of the lake.

The Legend of the Blue Water Stones

Forevermore

Under the midday sun, a warm summer breeze began to dance about, taking on its own shape. It danced upwards, then down, then to and fro, disturbing nothing in its path. The little breeze stretched wide and long and zipped though narrow spaces, making a whistling sound. The whistling sound caused it to dance more. And the more it danced, the more joyful it became. It was not long before it began to playfully lift leaves and tiny twigs off the ground, tossing them into the air. The little breeze traveled from North Point along the shoreline, rustling leaves and stirring sand particles as it went. When it reached Stony Point, it was strong enough to scatter leaves.

It touched down by Whisperleaf and whirled happily upwards, lifting Deweye into the warm summer air. Up he went, overjoyed, and calling to his friends, "Farewell! Farewell!"

> *"It is I, Dew-Eye!*
> *Light and Swift*
> *I spin, then fly*
> *And dream to drift*
> *In the summer sky*
> *The breeze will lift*
> *Me up so high*
> *What a an honor*
> *To be Dew-Eye!"*

He began to twirl and dance with immeasurable happiness as he was whisked away far above Whisperleaf. It was all he had ever hoped for, it was his true path. All of Stony Point wished him a farewell as they watched him vanish into the blue sky.

Even Solosong made a rare appearance as Deweye flew away, belting out his favorite song as he went. Solosong sat in Whisperleaf's highest leafless branch looking down at all the lake creatures. It was a fine day. Skeedad had returned with Daysee and Deweye and a stone named OldSkogmo, who had been gone since Whisperleaf was a young tree, many crow lifetimes.

Whisperleaf, stooped and brittle, called to her friend, "OldSkogmo? Is it really you? You have finally returned?"

At that very moment, the old stone awoke. He tipped forward a little as his eyes began to open wide. He blinked, looked around, then smiled a huge contented smile. It was as though his long slumber had only been for an instant. His smile faded slightly when he saw that his friend, Whisperleaf, was very old indeed and yet very grand in her wisdom.

"OldSkogmo, you see, I am quite old now and so very weary. I don't have much time left..." she said, as though reading his thoughts.

"Good friend Whisperleaf." It was all he could say. They were the first words he had uttered in many seasons. Skeedad and Daysee were elated to hear their friend finally speak.

All the lake creatures wanted to hear the tale of their journey. Skeedad and Daysee wanted to hear about OldSkogmo's travels and his days with Brookdweller and Mr. Littlejohn.

Everyone knew that OldSkogmo told things best of all. They began to gather around, hoping he would begin. The sun was already low in the sky. Solosong was quietly perched in Whisperleaf's uppermost branches.

The blue heron, the whitetail deer with her fawn and the geese had all returned in the final light of day.

And so, as the yellow sun dipped to the horizon, causing the sky to burst into orange and pink, then fade to dusky lavenders, OldSkogmo thought of all the tales he would tell. He watched reflectively as the moon appeared in the early night sky. He thought of Brookdweller, of Aunt Olive as a young girl, of the obstinate but good hearted Mr. Littlejohn,.

He thought of the times before the Drawer of Forgotten Things and of the days within it. He considered the persistence and kindliness of Lottie and goodScout, both unusual for their species. Then there was the unforgettable Deweye. Never had there been such a creature. And then, he thought of cheerful Daysee and of noble Skeedad. There were tales to tell about the world within a human dwelling and tales to tell about still other journeys. All the stories would be told. All the stories would keep for another time.

A hush fell over the lake creatures as OldSkogmo began to speak. He looked again to the giant yellow moon rising in the darkening sky, his eyes twinkling as though he were about to reveal a long awaited secret.

"Ahem! Listen carefully, dear friends. Many moon times ago, long, long before Solosong, long before Meadowsteps, Silverdew and even our friend, Blue Heron, it was our good fortune to know a young cottonwood tree who would come to be with us here on Stony Point beside the blue water forevermore.

Although young, she was quiet and kind and asked many wise questions. She grew strong and tall and over many winters bent closer and closer to the earth, sharing her wisdom with all who listened. In time, we began to call her Whisperleaf."

And so it was. As twilight blanketed the day, OldSkogmo told the legend of Whisperleaf's life as she stood nearby, old and bent, but filled with pride and joy because she knew she would live in their hearts forevermore. And it would always be good.

The End

© C. J. Clark

- 10 -

THE PERMANENCE OF WAVES

———————◯———————

The day they were to leave for Kansas, Olive was unable to find her grandfather. Lottie and Scout were gone, too. She'd been so preoccupied with packing the car that she'd lost track of time and had not noticed them slip away. Slip away? Did they slip away, or had they wandered off? Had they told her they were going somewhere together, or had they just gone?

She looked out the window. Her grandfather's car was still there, so was his bicycle. Someone was walking toward the cabin. She couldn't quite make out who it was, just that the person was carrying some sort of object. She watched as a young woman came into view. The woman looked so carefree, dressed in jeans and a warm sweater jacket for the brisk spring morning. For a moment, Olive thought she recognized the woman. Surely she wasn't coming to tell her some news about her grandfather's whereabouts. Olive felt a sense of dread come over her.

She flung open the door before the woman had a chance to knock, causing her to jump back and drop a large basket of muffins on the ground. The woman scrambled to pick up the rolling muffins while Olive stood watching her.

"Sorry…" Olive said.

"Goodness, you startled me! Olive?" The woman pushed her jacket hood back to reveal a disorganized mop of white blond hair. Her eyes were as blue as the sky and her face was rosy from the crisp morning air.

"Sorry. Yes, I'm Olive. Have we met?"

"Well, it's been a long, long time. But yes, I'm Matilda Peterson. Our family's cabin is down by the creek." She pointed vaguely toward the woods. "You and I used to play together during summer vacations when we were kids." Seeing Olive's hesitation, she added, "It was really an awfully long time ago."

"Oh yes. Matilda," Olive said uncertainly. "I'm so sorry. It's good to see you again. Come in, come in." She stood back, opening the door wide, embarrassed at her own lack of hospitality.

"Oh well, thanks but I can't stay. I was just bringing your grandfather some muffins I baked this morning. They're blueberry, his favorite." Matilda continued standing on the front step and handed the basket of remaining muffins to Olive.

"You know, I can't find him this morning," Olive said suddenly looking toward the driveway, oblivious to the fact that Matilda had awkwardly shifted the spilled muffins to her other hand.

"What do you mean?" Matilda raised her eyebrows slightly.

"It's just that we are driving back to Kansas today, and I've been packing the car. I didn't notice him leave or remember either of them say anything about going anywhere. His dog is gone, too."

"Scout?" Matilda gasped. The missing dog seemed to alarm her. She put her free hand to her mouth.

"I really don't even know how long they've been gone. I'd wanted Grandpa to come back with us to Kansas. He's getting up there in years, you know, and I've been concerned about him being up here all alone. He's so frail. I guess I've just been so preoccupied with that. I don't know." She looked toward the driveway again.

Matilda followed Olive's gaze, then laughed. "Frail? I never thought of him as frail. We can barely keep up with your grandpa. He's an amazing man."

"I'm really pretty worried," Olive said, ignoring Matilda's comment.

"I'm sure he's fine. Don't you think they just went for a little walk or something?" Matilda answered.

"I don't know. I guess. I'd probably better go look for them though." Olive wondered why Matilda seemed so unconcerned. Sure her grandfather was an amazing man, but he was an old man nonetheless. He could fall or get lost or have a sudden heart attack or any number of mishaps. It was up to her to protect him, wasn't it? She just wanted Matilda to leave.

"Thanks so much for the muffins. Here, let me throw those away." She reached for the stray muffins that Matilda was still holding.

"Okay. Look, if you can't find him let us know. Our phone number is right next to his phone. He wrote it on the wall, actually. I'm sure he's just fine. Maybe if you wait a little while, they'll be back." Matilda turned to go and added, "Nice seeing you again. Next time you're here, come down for coffee. You're always welcome."

Olive barely heard this. She felt as though she was colliding with a world where it was no big deal when people wandered off without a word to anyone and where it was okay for old people to live alone with no one around for miles. A world where freshly baked blueberry muffins arrived at your doorstep with great nonchalance marked by references to the past and vague invitations for the future. She waved at Matilda, then went back inside to find her hiking boots. She had to unpack her suitcase to find them. As she was crisscrossing the shoelaces, she wondered if she might be overreacting. Maybe Matilda was right. She should wait a bit. They might return at any moment.

She stepped outside just as a noisy flock of Canadian geese soared high above her in the light blue sky. She watched as a few of the geese broke the V formation. Their flight looked suddenly jumbled and disorganized. And yet they continued on, in their forward direction, honking loudly.

Olive inhaled deeply. At that moment she felt there was nothing more exhilarating in the world than a crisp cool Minnesota morning in the heart of Otter Tail County. She felt energized. What could it hurt to go look for her grandfather and niece? And besides, what if they were in trouble? If he had only told her where they were going, she wouldn't have to wonder.

She followed the long winding driveway to Stony Point Trail and then stopped. Which way should she go? She tried to think like her grandfather, then smiled to herself realizing how impossible that would be. Someday, somehow, she decided right then and there, she would spend more time up here in these north woods. She would learn everything her grandfather knew, all the things he had tried to teach her over the years. She would ask him to tell her his stories again. He was such a wonderful storyteller.

Years ago he'd shown her a trail through the deep woods that he'd marked with pieces of painted rope tied around tree trunks. She'd been fascinated with the trail's twists and turns through underbrush and ravines, how tall the trees were, how dark it became the deeper into the woods they went. Then the sunlight would peek through as they reached a partial clearing. She would feel like heaven itself had opened to them. Never once had she felt uneasy. Her grandfather knew the way. He was the smartest, most capable man she had ever known. A momentary pang of grief filled her heart as she thought of him helpless and lost in these same woods.

Olive cut across Stony Point Trail into the woods, careful to step high over a sagging barbed wire fence. She noticed a tree with a piece of red painted rope tied around it. Confident that this was the old trail, she set out to find the next tree marker. It wasn't exactly as she'd remembered it. There were trees down and decaying from a tornado that had ripped through the area a year before. One of the trees lay on the ground like a fallen soldier with its red rope marker still tied to it. Downed trees obscured the tiny path, and she had to look hard into the woods for the next trail markers.

She stood staring for a moment feeling almost blinded by the monotony of tree trunks and under-brush. When she finally spotted a marker, she noticed another one several feet ahead of it and still another as the path took a turn into a sort of low grassy area. She stepped over a huge fallen moss-covered tree, startling a black squirrel who scampered out to scold her. Three white-tailed deer bounded ahead of her, disturbed by her presence. She watched as they disappeared into the deep woods, amazed at how quietly they escaped her view.

Her grandfather had often told her that time stood still in the woods. Not the time of day or time of year, but the idea of time itself. Olive had paid little attention to his words then. But now, alone on this unfamiliar trail, she understood fully what he'd meant, and it amazed her. She meandered along picking up her pace when she spotted another marker.

At first it seemed curious that the painted rope color had been changed to green, but she decided that he must have run out of the red paint. The green was harder to see and the trail became nearly nonexistent. Just when she thought she'd lost the path, it would reappear and there would be another green rope marker to identify it. It was odd though. Olive didn't quite remember the trail leading into a more sparse birch woods, nor did she remember it cutting through tall reeds and cattails along the back water of the lake. At one point, she came so close to the water that she frightened a flock of mallards that rushed upwards, squawking angrily.

Then it dawned on her that something was terribly wrong. The trail markers were further and further apart. Some weren't even painted. It disturbed her to think that perhaps her grandfather had wandered out here aimlessly marking a trail that led nowhere. She'd been more worried about his aging physical condition than his mental capacities. He'd always been sharp as a tack, an articulate thinker. Was it possible that his mind was becoming clouded and dulled with age?

Olive continued onward in the direction that seemed most likely to her. She glanced up at the sky, trying to determine time of day and direction. How long had she been following this trail? There were over a hundred acres of woods all around her. Could Lottie and her grandfather be just up ahead? Deep inside she felt a whirl of panic begin to rise. She started to turn back, but everything looked the same. Refusing to give in to the panic, she stopped. Okay, so I'm a little turned around. This shouldn't be difficult. I can do this, she thought.

Suddenly a memory of her mother swimming ahead of her in the lake took hold of her. The lake water shimmered in the bright sunlight. Her mother was wearing her favorite blue one-piece bathing suit, which made her creamy white skin appear even more blanched. Her white bathing cap with the little yellow flowers made her look like an egghead. She swam easily, kicking her legs, swimming further and further away. She rolled onto her back and bobbed up and down in the waves, motioning for Olive to follow. Wait, wait for me, Mother. But the memory faded, and Olive was alone again in the woods. Her mother had always loved the water more than the woods.

Olive closed her eyes and thought about the waves caused by her mother's swimming rolling into the shore against the blue water stones. A wind was beginning to stir the treetops and a chill had returned to the air. As if she could will herself to find her way back, she visualized the blue water stones along the beach. She decided to walk into the wind. Even as she did this, the dull sound of a barking dog sounded far in the distance.

"Scout? Scout! Scout! Scout!" she yelled. Somehow her shouting seemed ridiculously futile. She stopped abruptly. She began to walk briskly toward the direction of the barking dog, listening so intently that she lost her footing. She tripped and fell forward, landing face down in a bramble of spiky underbrush. Olive wanted to cry. How could this be possible? She couldn't be lost. She didn't bother to get up for a long time.

When she did get up, she discovered that her jeans were ripped and her left shin was lacerated and bleeding.

She groaned. With her shirt sleeve, she mopped at the blood oozing from her wound. As she did this, she realized that the barking dog sounded even closer than before. When Olive stood up, a pain shot through her leg. She gained her footing by leaning heavily on a large cottonwood tree. She listened. Was it her imagination or was the dog coming closer?

"Scout! Scout!" she shouted. Just then it occurred to her that maybe the barking dog wasn't Scout. Maybe it was some rangy vicious wild dog. Or a wolf. Was that possible? Wolves? In Otter Tail County? She laughed out loud, but then stopped, shuddering slightly when she remembered the coyotes she'd heard howling in the night. She put her head in her hands. I've got to get a grip here, she thought.

There was a faint rustling in the nearby underbrush. Olive took shallow breaths, covering her eyes with her hands.

"Olive?"

"Grandpa?" Olive jerked her head up to see Scout bounding over to her, her grandfather and Lottie close behind. They were coming from the opposite direction, which made Olive feel disoriented. Had she found them or had they found her?

"Aunt Olive, what are you doing way out here?" Lottie asked, clearly puzzled. "Oh my gosh, what happened to your leg?"

But her grandfather had already begun to apply a makeshift bandage to Olive's leg. "It looks superficial. We need to get you back so we can clean this up." He took her by the arm and led her forward, testing her ability to bear weight.

"Wait. Wait. This is nuts. You shouldn't be helping me. I came out here looking for you three." She looked from her grandfather to Lottie to Scout. They looked fine. It was obvious they were not lost and that they had not been lost at all.

"Looking for us? Well for heaven's sake, why," her grandfather asked, truly astonished.

"I couldn't find you anywhere, Grandpa. When I was finished packing the car, I looked for you. I was pretty worried, because, you know…" Olive hesitated. It all seemed foolish now. She was the one who was lost and injured, and they were the ones helping her find the way back.

"Well, I'm sure sorry, Olive," her grandfather said.

"But I followed your old trail markers. The rope color changed from red to green and then there were some that weren't painted any color at all. It was confusing." Olive brushed bramble twigs from her hair.

"Green," her grandfather said thoughtfully, stroking his chin. "The green rope marks an old game trail. The red markers are the hiking path. You must've taken a wrong turn. You wandered way off course."

Olive moaned. Of course. He had marked two trails. She shook her head, not knowing what to say.

"Grandpa was showing me the big birdhouses he made for the herons. They're gigantic," Lottie said.

"We were just across the road in the woods…not far at all. I'm surprised you didn't see us," her grandfather added. He took his cap off and placed it on Olive's head the way he had when she was a little girl.

Olive patted the cap into place and laughed. Here was her grandfather coming to her rescue. Why had she been so worried about him? He was as solid and constant as he had ever been.

For the rest of her days, Olive would remember this moment. And she would always remember driving away with Lottie, smiling and waving good-bye to her hero, her great grandpa, standing beside the cabin, old

and bent but wise and capable, with Scout by his side.
She would look past him at the waves rolling steadily
into shore, splashing over his blue water stones,
memorizing it all.

The Permanence of Waves
was written for all ages.

The drawings are submitted
in remembrance of the
author's childhood at Stony Point.

Drawings by C.J. Clark

DRAWINGS BY C.J. CLARK

To Order this Book

The Permanence of Waves

If not available at your favorite bookstore,
order from

LangMarc Publishing

P.O. Box 90488 • Austin, Texas 78709-0488
1-800-864-1648
www.langmarc.com • e-mail: langmarc@booksails.com

- -

Please send payment with order:

_____ copies of *The Permanence of Waves*
     at $14.95   _____
Sales tax (Texas residents only) 8.25%   _____
Shipping $2.50 1 book; $1 additional books _____
Amount of check enclosed: _____

Or Credit card: _____
Expires: _____ small 3-4 digit no: ____

Your name: _____

Address: _____

_____

Phone number: _____
e-mail: _____

For prints or books you may contact

C. J. Clark

cjclark144@att.net
1420 Cypress Creek Road, Ste. 200-144
Cedar Park, Texas 78613

LaVergne, TN USA
25 August 2010
194607LV00002B/9/A